# BAD BOY'S SECRET BABY

NATASHA L. BLACK

# INTRODUCTION

**I have to tell him.**
**But this secret could destroy us both.**

He's still the same rebel that had me begging for his touch,
But now he's got money and power.
What he doesn't have is the truth - the life changing secret
I've been keeping for years.

Now he's back and determined to make me his.

It's not easy being the sheriff's little sister in this small town,
Especially when the sheriff practically hates his former best
friend.

**Will the secrets of our past destroy us all?**
**I suppose there's one way to find out.**

## JACOB

I t had been years, eight years to be exact, since I'd darkened the door of Burning Butte, North Dakota. I had thought things would have changed dramatically. I had. The small town had not. I stared out the heavily tinted driver's-side window of my Ford F-350 and saw the ice cream shop was still in the same place. On the other side of the street was what I thought had to be the tiniest bookstore in the world. Most of the buildings were A-frames. The northern town got a lot of snow in the winter, and the buildings with the flat roofs always suffered. I could see there were still a few holding up, but I imagined it was only a matter of time before they were demolished under the weight of the snow.

The businesses lined the main road through town, all vying for that prime piece of real estate. I passed the Old Flame Saloon and grinned. It was amazing that place was still operating. Of course, not that surprising. The bar was one of two in town, where everyone went to get a drink. The other tavern was more of a restaurant and was always packed with families with mommies and daddies who wanted to drink but were also stuck with the kids. Parents could pretend to be getting in some family time while throwing back a few beers.

I kept my speed slow as I rolled through the small town, taking it all in. It felt good to be back. It felt even better to be back in my new position. I wasn't the same kid who'd been run out of town by the local sheriff all those years ago. I was a man. A man with money and power. Not a lot of either, but a hell of a lot more than what I had when I'd left.

I was back and I was determined to show Sheriff Arthur Maxwell I wasn't the kind of man who allowed himself to be pushed around anymore. I dared him to try and pull the same bullshit he did back then. I was back and I was determined as hell to prove I wasn't a worthless piece of trash from the wrong side of town with no future. There had been other adjectives used to describe me, but they didn't matter. I was going to prove them all wrong.

I drove through town, heading out to the outskirts where Western Energies had set up shop. There were a few houses on sprawling farmland dotting the area with green pastures and cows lazily grazing as the road bent to the right. The old warehouse that had been used as a feedstore didn't even look the same. I wouldn't have known it had ever been a warehouse if I hadn't seen it with my own eyes as a kid. I was surprised to see the old, decrepit buildings that had once dotted the barren land gone and replaced by a paved parking lot. The old buildings that once stood in the area were dangerous, more of an attraction for kids to get up to no good. Like me. I was one of those kids, drinking and partying and doing other things I shouldn't have.

I drove through the smooth parking lot, looking for a spot close to the door, and was surprised to see my name on a sign in front of a spot near the door.

"Well, look at that," I cooed. "Reserved for Jacob Miner, Vice President of Western Energies," I read aloud, unable to stop smiling as I pulled my truck into the spot.

I threw it into park, grabbed my phone, and hopped out of the truck, smoothing down the dark polo shirt with the Western Energies logo on the upper left. I'd worn a pair of nice jeans for my first day. I bent down to check my reflection in the side mirror, making sure my hair was in place. I hadn't been able to resist driving down the highway with my window down and the music blaring. I used my fingertips to comb back my short brown hair before standing to my full six-two height again.

I strode up the couple of steps to the front doors and walked into the sleek, modern building that looked completely out of place in the old mining town. There was muted lighting throughout the lobby that was covered with tasteful, modern art and several little seating areas arranged around the wide-open space. It was like something one would expect to see in a big city, not a little out of the way town like Burning Butte. A receptionist was sitting behind a tall desk, a headset on her head as she smiled at me.

"Hi, I'm Jacob Miner, here to see Larry Welsh," I said in a friendly tone.

"Yes, Mr. Miner, he's expecting you. I'll take you in," she said, sliding off the tall chair she'd been sitting in.

She came around the edge of the reception desk. Her attire, a very attractive business suit with heels that could be used as a lethal weapon, were starkly different than the flowing dresses and jean-clad women I had seen on my drive through town. I imagined she must stick out like a sore thumb if she ever dared shop at one of the local shops.

The cement floor of the building was finished with a marble appearance and a high shine so perfect it was like walking on a mirror. She turned a corner and strode toward a set of double doors at the end of the hall. She knocked once before turning the handle and pushing the door open, gesturing for me to go inside.

"Thank you," I said with a nod before strolling into the office with a big black-and-gray rug spread over the cement. Larry Welsh was sitting behind a massive cherrywood desk lining one side of the office. The guy was a younger version of George Clooney. He was a handsome, suave dude that could charm just about anyone. He was wealthy and it showed in the way he dressed, but he also had that Texas charm about him that made him approachable and well liked.

My new boss and the owner of Western Energies got to his feet. "Jacob! Good to see you. I take it you found the place okay."

I chuckled. "It's not hard to find. This place is amazing. I can't believe the transformation," I told him, still in awe of how the old feed warehouse had been turned into something out of *Architectural Digest*.

"Thank you. It's been a long process, but my design team really pulled off a miracle. Have a seat," he said, gesturing to one of the two leather couches facing each other on either side of the massive rug.

I sat down, resting my ankle on my knee, and looked around the grand office. It exuded wealth and power. "This is really nice," I told him again.

"Thank you, I'm excited for our future here. We're going to do great things together. I think Fate had a hand in the two of us meeting back in Chicago. I had been looking for somewhere just like this to invest in, and you pointed me in the right direction," he said with a small laugh.

I shrugged a shoulder, thinking back to the event that had been held for energy company execs and owners. It was a networking event, rubbing elbows, shaking hands, and making connections that would make the wealthy a little wealthier. I didn't mind having a role in that. My goal was to be wealthy and powerful and prove to everyone I wasn't a worthless punk kid. I had worked my ass off in school to earn my bachelor's degree in business management. That event had been the ticket I needed to get a foothold in the world that would make me successful. A single, casual conversation with a guy had led to me becoming the VP of a major energy company.

Larry had jumped at the chance to hire me when he found where I was from. The oil boom in the Dakotas was big money for those willing to take the risk with an investment. I had the in Larry was looking for. Between my knowledge of the area and his business savvy, we'd decided to make it happen and now, here we were.

I had gone through all the training at his Dallas offices with the intention of coming home to Burning Butte to work as VP. It couldn't have worked out any better if I tried. It was exactly what I had intended to do when I'd been very unceremoniously run out of town eight long years ago. I was back. I was back to reclaim what had been taken from me. I loved that I was coming back home with a fancy title and a six-figure salary to go with it.

"I have to admit I thought things would have changed some. It is almost exactly like I remember. I guess time doesn't move quite as fast here," I chuckled.

He grinned, slapping his knee. "That's going to work out in our favor. We're about to shake things up and bring this town into the twenty-first century with good paying jobs and all the benefits that brings. We'll get new businesses in town and infuse life back into this sleepy little place."

I grimaced. "We're going to have to do it with a great deal of finesse. These people are old-school, and they might not be all that open to change," I warned him.

"I'm prepared for that. You're my secret weapon. I'm counting on you to help soothe those ruffled feathers," he said, that old-boy smile in place. "Let me show you your office," he said, getting to his feet.

My office was in the exact opposite direction of his down an identical hallway. I was impressed to see that it had the same double doors. He pushed open the door, grinning from ear to ear as he stepped out of the way and let me walk in. I was thoroughly impressed.

"Wow. This is nice," I said, taking in the luxurious furnishings and the fluffy, dark rug that added a little warmth to the stark office.

There were built-in shelves lining one wall and a desk that was similar to the one in his office. I could already picture a piece of art I'd had my eye on for some time hanging on the huge blank wall behind my desk. It was a little dark, but it exuded luxury. I liked it. It was what I had always dreamed of.

"Only the best for my favorite vice president," he said.

"Thank you, Larry. This is great. I look forward to making this a successful venture for you and the company," I told him.

"What are you doing tonight?" he asked.

I shrugged a shoulder. "I've got a room at the local inn. I'm thinking I'll dine on some vending machine snacks and maybe a Big Mac," I said with a laugh.

He slapped a hand on my shoulder. "Why don't you come by the house tonight for dinner. I'd like you to meet the family."

I nodded, not about to turn down a hot meal and the chance to cement the friendship between Larry and me. He was a good guy. I had interviewed with a lot of other companies, but I didn't like the vibe, or the CEO was not the kind of person I would ever want to be associated with.

"I'd like that, thank you."

He quickly gave me his address. I should have known. He had the biggest house in the damn county. I was going to start looking for my own house ASAP. I wished I had the time to have something built, but I needed a place to rest my head now, not in a year. I had a Realtor working on the problem and was hoping to be moved into a new place by the end of the week. The inn was not exactly my idea of a homecoming.

# 2

## ERIN

I loved the kitchen in the Welsh mansion. What wasn't to love? It was huge and bright and had counter space for days. It was a gourmet kitchen well thought out, which made cooking an absolute dream. It was the kitchen a real cook would absolutely go gaga over. The entire house on sprawling acreage outside of town was stunning. It had been built with about a million custom details to make it super comfortable and fancy by a megastar who thought he was going to retire to the country and have a cattle ranch. The guy lived in the house for a couple of weeks before he figured out he wasn't a rancher and country living wasn't for him. All of us in town knew it was the Dakota winter that sealed the deal. Only the toughest and most resilient could survive one of those.

The house had sat empty for years until the Welsh family came along. Now, it was a happy, family home getting put to good use, and I got to call the place home as well. It had taken me close to a month to learn the layout. There were about a million doors, and it was easy to get lost inside the sprawling home.

"Can I have the blue crayon?" Mitchell Welsh asked my daughter, Ellie.

I glanced over my shoulder to make sure all three of the kids were behaving themselves. My little girl had immediately taken to Mitchell and Mackenzie Welsh, my two young charges. They all got along really well, and it made my job as a nanny so much easier. I loved that I could work and have my seven-year-old daughter with me.

When the Welshes moved to town six months ago and put out an ad looking for a nanny, I jumped at the chance. Ellie and Mackenzie were both in the same grade, and Mitchell was just a year younger, which made it nice. They could all play together and keep one another occupied while I did things like cook dinner.

"You guys play nice," I warned when I heard some grumbling coming from the table where they were all supposed to be drawing me a picture of their favorite thing.

"Mom, Mitchell has all the blue crayons," Ellie complained.

"Mitchell, share please," I said without turning around.

Thankfully, they were all good kids and the squabbles were minor and limited. When I had taken the job, I had been worried Ellie wouldn't get along with the other kids or that the Welsh kids would be spoiled little monsters that were too difficult to take care of. They weren't. They were great, and my life had changed for the better. I was finally able to move out of my father's house as part of the job included an apartment over the four-car garage. It was my own little space with my daughter, something we had never had the luxury of enjoying in the past.

"Guys, in about three minutes, it's going to be time to start on those homework sheets. Put away the crayons please," I told them.

"But I'm not done," Ellie whined.

"Three minutes," I said again.

There were some muted complaints, but I wasn't worried they wouldn't do what they were told. They usually did with minimal resistance. I covered the lasagna and slid it in the oven before turning to the long center island to finish chopping the veggies for the salad I had made to go with it. I loved cooking and taking care of a big family. Back home, I used to make dinner for my dad and sometimes my brother.

That was another perk to living way out in the country: my brother wasn't always in my face with his buddies beside him. I loved my brother, but damn, did he get on my nerves. It seemed like he was convinced he was my father and was constantly lecturing me and trying to tell me how to raise my daughter and how to live in general. Getting away from him had certainly helped our relationship.

I tossed the cherry tomatoes on the salad, covered it with plastic wrap, and stuck it in the huge double-door refrigerator to chill while the lasagna cooked. I quickly washed my hands and moved to the table where the kids were cleaning up the crayons.

"All right, who's ready to play a little game?" I teased.

"Me!" they all yelled in unison.

I checked the time and realized Mrs. Welsh had been gone a while. She'd gone in search of "appropriately sophisticated wine" to go with the lasagna. Poor Mrs. Welsh was struggling to adjust to country living. She was used to the finer things in life, like Broadway shows, five-star restaurants, and spas whenever she felt like it. Living in the country had been a huge change for her, but she seemed to be handling it well.

"Okay, everyone on your feet and get in a line," I directed the kids.

They all scrambled out of their chairs and lined up in the spacious kitchen area. The table was more of a craft play area than an actual eating area. The Welshes preferred to eat in the formal dining room. In fact, I considered the kitchen mostly my area. Mrs. Welsh wasn't a huge fan of cooking in general.

I started the kids on a little math facts game. It got them up and helped worked out the wiggles before dinner while brushing up on their math. I had thought at one point that I wanted to be a teacher. I went to school and got my Associate's degree in early childhood education, but raising Ellie on my own had made school difficult. I didn't want to spend so much time away from her and had decided to put it on hold until she was a little older. I had been working in daycare facilities in order to keep her with me while earning enough money to support us. Even then, I was still stuck living in my dad's house.

I heard the door open and close and assumed Mrs. Welsh was back from her wine hunt. The heavy footsteps told me otherwise. It was Mr. Welsh, which meant he would be ready for dinner. He liked to eat around the same time every night. Sometimes Ellie and I joined the family, but generally, dinner was my time with Ellie alone. We usually did puzzles, played one of her video games, or read. People often asked if I missed having a life, but in my opinion, I had a better life than most. I loved my little girl.

"All right, guys, head outside to play. You've got fifteen minutes, and then it will be time to wash up," I told them.

"We get lasagna!" Ellie cheered, clapping her hands before racing out the French doors that opened into a backyard that was essentially a private playground for the kids with damn near every toy imaginable.

Mr. Welsh walked into the kitchen; his nose turned up as he smelled the air. "Is that lasagna?" he asked.

I smiled. "It is."

"Thank you. I think we'll have to give you a raise. You know you're not expected to cook and clean," he said with a friendly smile.

"I don't mind. I like cooking, especially in this kitchen," I told him.

"Is my wife in?" he asked.

"No, she ran to the store in search of wine to go with dinner."

He nodded. "I have a guest coming for dinner tonight. I assume there is plenty?"

I softly laughed. "You know there always is. I make enough for a small army."

"Great. I have a conference call. I'll be in my study," he said and walked out of the kitchen.

I figured I had better get the table set, knowing Mr. Welsh was likely entertaining a potential investor. I wanted him to succeed. I liked my job and I liked the family and didn't want his business to fail and them to leave town. I grabbed the dishes and carried them into the dining room, setting it in a semi-formal style. As I walked past the windows facing the backyard, I checked on the kids before grabbing another load of dishes and the necessary condiments and carrying them back into the dining room.

I heard the doorbell ring just as I was pulling out the lasagna from the oven. I quickly put it on the stove, deposited the oven mitts on the counter, and headed for the foyer. Mrs. Welsh wasn't home, and Mr. Welsh was on the phone. That left me to act as head of the house or butler, one of the many hats I wore.

I opened the door, prepared to greet the dinner guest, and froze. My eyes had to be playing tricks on me. There was no way Jacob Miner was standing on the other side of the door. I blinked, wondering why I had conjured him up after all these years.

He was looking at me with complete shock. I imagined I probably had a similar expression. "Jacob?" I breathed the word, the sound barely audible.

I couldn't believe he was standing there. He was three feet in front of me looking handsome as ever. No, more handsome. He was a man now. He had those same hazel eyes that could flash blue to green with his mood. There were a few wrinkles at the corners of his eyes, but they were so much the same. His light brown hair was cut short, much shorter than it had been in the days we'd been together. There was the slightest hint of stubble on the stern jawline, giving him a rugged yet sexy look that was making my belly feel very warm.

He was staring at me, and the surprise at seeing me was evident on his face. I had a flashback to the last time I'd seen him. Neither of us had known I was pregnant at the time. One day, he was gone without a word. When I had found out I was pregnant, I had no idea where to even look for him. His cell phone had been shut off, and no one around town knew where he'd disappeared to. It didn't take me long to figure out I was going to be a single mom. At that point, I decided to keep the identify of my baby's daddy a secret.

"Erin Maxwell." He said my full name as if he wasn't sure it was really me.

His voice rolled over me, sparking more memories. I remembered what it felt like to be in his strong arms, his body over mine. I remembered everything. The way he had tasted, the softness of his lips and the hardness of his body. Staring at him now, I suspected he was far more solid than he had been in his youth. It sent me down a dangerous path as I remembered our last time together. We'd snuck out and lain together under the stars.

I heard a squeal come from the backyard. My initial reaction was it was just the kids having fun. A split second later I went into full panic as I stared at the man who'd fathered my child and had no idea. My eyes widened and my heartbeat picked up. I debated slamming the door in his face but remembered he was Mr. Welsh's guest.

# 3

JACOB

It was the moment I had been waiting for. Eight long years I had thought about what it would be like to see the woman who had stolen my heart back when I was young and dumb. I had always planned to come back. I had so much to say to her. Over the years, I had hoped the feelings would fade. I hoped I could move on and never think about Erin Maxwell again. I had convinced myself the only reason I wanted to see her one more time was to show her I had amounted to someone. Seeing her again was not what I had expected. It was like a punch to the gut. She was beautiful. Her dark hair, a chestnut hue, looked silky, and I could almost smell the fruity shampoo she always used. She looked the same but prettier, more like a woman than the teenager I had been dreaming about for years.

I could feel her surprise at seeing me. It mimicked my own. While I had every intention of seeing her again, I hadn't expected it to be right then. It was the culmination of eight years of longing to rest my eyes upon her, hear her whiskey-smooth voice, and smell that unique scent that was hers alone.

"What are you doing here?" she asked, her head slowly shaking back and forth.

"I was invited to din—" Realization slammed into me. Erin had answered the door of the Welsh house.

I had this strange idea she would be single. Why? Why would she have been single? I was staring at one of the most beautiful women in the world. She would of course be married. But married to my boss?

"Dinner?" she finished.

I blinked at her. "Yes, dinner. Larry invited me to dinner."

She slowly nodded her head. "I see."

I felt pure rage burn through my veins. The very thought of Larry touching the woman I had come back to Burning Butte to win back made me sick. I wanted to shout and pound on my chest with my fists. I would burn Western Energies to the damn ground if necessary. I wanted my woman. I had gone through hell to get my ass in a position to come back to get her, and I was not about to give up so easily. Jealousy had reared its ugly head, and all I could think about was reclaiming what I had lost. Or given up. I wasn't going to lose Erin again, not without one hell of a fight.

Erin stepped back; her arm outstretched as she gestured for me to enter the home. "Come in. There's a sitting room off to the right. Make yourself comfortable. Larry is on the phone, but he'll be right out," she said in a stiff tone.

Before she could say anything more, a blonde woman walked up to the door, wearing a tight skirt and a button-up shirt with a lacy bra peeking through the unbuttoned top. She took one look at me and smiled.

"Hi," she said, a bright smile with perfectly straight veneers exploding across her face. "Is this your friend?" she asked Erin.

Erin shook her head. "No."

"I'm here at Larry's request," I said, still not sure who the woman was.

"Well, I'm Mrs. Welsh. I'm assuming you're the new VP he's been talking up.

I looked at Erin, who was staring at me with such confusion I actually took a step back. "I'm Jacob Miner," I said with a friendly smile.

"You can call me Ivy. I see you've met our nanny. I just stepped out to grab some wine to go with our dinner. You wouldn't think it would be such a difficult task, but I assure you it is ridiculous," she carried on.

"Actually, I know Erin. We've known each other for years," I said, looking back at Erin, who was looking at me with hurt and anger in her eyes.

I felt like an asshole. I had jumped to conclusions, and they were all the wrong ones. "I'll let Mr. Welsh know you're here," Erin said, stepping around me and practically running down the hall.

. I turned to look back at Mrs. Welsh, who was eying me like

I was a piece of meat at the market. I was waiting for her to reach out and squeeze me.

"Why don't you follow me?" Mrs. Welsh said with the same flirty smile. "We can break into this wine and see if it's any good."

She walked past me, expecting me to follow. I did. She was a beautiful woman, but she wasn't what I wanted. I wanted Erin, and she was the reason I was back in Burning Butte. I had so much I wanted to say and explain to her. She was my sole focus.

I followed Ivy into the kitchen, and I was a little taken aback by the sheer size of it. There were two refrigerators and two stoves and about three miles of counter space. She opened a drawer and pulled out a corkscrew.

"Jacob, you made it!" Larry's voice boomed through the house.

I turned and smiled. "It's not hard to miss this place," I joked.

"Do you like it?"

"What's not to like? This wasn't here when I lived here," I told him.

"Why don't we go into the dining room and let Ivy finish up in here," Larry suggested. "I've got a few matters I'd like to discuss."

"Sure," I said, following him through an archway.

"Larry Welsh, this is a casual dinner, don't you dare talk shop all night," Ivy pouted.

"I can eat, drink, and talk all at the same time dear," Larry quipped without turning back to look at her.

I caught the look of disappointment on Ivy's face, offering her a smile before continuing behind my boss.

My eyes scanned the area, looking for a glimpse of Erin. Larry was chatting away, talking about the house and how they'd found the property and on and on. I was barely listening. I made the appropriate sounds, nodding my head as we walked into the formal dining room with a table that could probably sit twelve. I wondered how many kids the Welshes had; it had never come up in our conversations and I didn't remember seeing any family pictures in Larry's office.

"Have a seat," he said, gesturing to one of the dark wood chairs.

Larry moved to the sidebar and pulled the cork on a glass decanter. He poured two glasses of what I assumed was scotch before coming to sit down at the table. I took the glass and sipped the strong liquor, my mind on Erin and the hundreds of things I wanted to say to her. I had practiced what I would say when I saw her over and over, and now that I was within a few feet of her, I couldn't think straight let alone speak.

"Thank you," I mumbled, remembering my manners.

"How was your first day back home?" Larry asked with a smile.

I offered him a smile in return. "Interesting, although I haven't seen much just yet."

"You will, you will. Did you get the name of that realtor I sent?"

"I did," I answered, my mind still not focused on the conversation.

"Great. You just let me know what you need, and I'll make sure you get yourself a house right away. A little cash has a way of greasing the wheels if you know what I mean," he said with a wink.

"I do. Thank you," I said.

I couldn't wait until I could become an official homeowner in Burning Butte. Erin's brother and father weren't going to run me out of town quite so easily this time. I wasn't a naïve, kid who didn't have the confidence to stand up to the town bullies. I didn't care if they were holding badges. I was a law-abiding citizen, and there wasn't shit they could do to keep me out of town.

Ivy bustled in carrying a large dish and put it down on the table. "I hope you like lasagna. Our nanny is the best. She made dinner tonight."

"I love lasagna," I answered, a little surprised to know Erin had cooked.

I remembered how much she hated cooking when she was a kid. With her mother gone, Erin had kind of been thrust into the role of the lady of the house. She was stuck taking care of her father and brother whether she wanted to or not. Cooking was not a chore she had loved.

"Let me go get the kids settled and we can have dinner," Ivy said, walking out of the dining room.

I wondered why the nanny wasn't taking care of the kids. "Will you excuse me for a second?" I asked Larry.

"Sure, sure. Bathroom is out the door and down on the left," he said, staring at his phone.

"Thank you," I said and left the table.

I wanted to find Erin. I couldn't exactly go roaming around the big house, but I was hoping I would run into her. This wasn't exactly how I planned our reunion going. I needed her to see I was there for her and her alone. The job was just a means to that end. I found the bathroom and waited a few minutes before walking back out and taking the long way back to the dining room. I never saw her. I took my seat at the table with Ivy across from me and Larry at the head of the table, trying to hide my disappointment.

"Will your family be joining us?" I asked, hoping it meant the nanny would also be eating dinner with us.

"No, they ate in the kitchen and are upstairs playing before it's time for bed," Ivy answered.

I smiled, nodding my head as I took a bite of lasagna. It was amazingly good. Erin had become quite the cook. Maybe she would cook dinner for me one day soon.

"Please tell the Erin I found her food delicious," I commented.

"Of course. She is amazing. We were so lucky to have found her when we moved out here. I was worried we were going to have to try and find someone from the city and move them with us. I can't imagine there would be a lot of young ladies willing to live in this small town. The nightlife must be so boring here," Ivy said, clearly aghast.

I chuckled, taking a sip of the scotch. "Trust me, there is plenty to do, but it is probably not quite the same as one of the dance clubs in the city. Country folks have a way of finding their own entertainment," I assured her, thinking back to the rowdy parties and silly, sometimes ridiculously stupid things we had done for excitement.

## 4

ERIN

M y heart was racing as I threw my car in reverse and backed out of the garage. The Welshes had been kind enough to give me my own slot in the massive building. I was still reeling from my encounter with Jacob. He was my boss's new VP apparently? My head was a flurry of broken thoughts and old memories floating to the surface. It made it difficult to think straight, but I knew I had to get away from there with Ellie.

"Mom, I thought we were going to have lasagna," Ellie whined from the back seat.

"I changed my mind. We're going to have dinner with Grandpa instead," I said in a cheerful tone.

"But you said we were going to have lasagna," she repeated.

I sighed, looking in the rearview mirror and feeling a little guilty. "I'm sorry, sweetie. Plans changed. Don't you want to see Grandpa?" I asked hopefully.

Ellie shrugged a shoulder. I knew she loved my dad. He'd

been a huge part of her life. I felt bad for up and leaving the kids with Ivy, but I was technically off at six and I didn't feel like sticking around and eating dinner with the guy who'd broken my heart all those years ago. I also didn't want him to see Ellie. Jacob wasn't an idiot. It wouldn't take him long to figure out the math and realize she was his. That would surely lead to a very uncomfortable conversation I didn't want to have in front of Ellie or my bosses.

I pulled into the driveway of my childhood home where my father still lived, and sighed. I wasn't looking forward to a lot of questions and hoped he wouldn't ask. Ellie and I knocked once before heading inside.

"Dad?" I called out.

"In the kitchen," he hollered.

I could hear the beeping of the microwave and guessed he was popping in his dinner. "Hey," I said, noticing the TV dinner in his hand.

"Busted." He grinned.

"You know those aren't really a meal," I lectured.

"I heated up some leftovers to go with it. That's a meal," he reasoned.

"I'll make you something to eat."

"What brings my two favorite ladies by?" he asked, giving Ellie a big hug.

"We just thought it was time for a visit," I answered nonchalantly.

He gave me a look that said he knew I wasn't giving him the

full truth, but fortunately didn't push it. That was part of the problem of living with a cop all your life. They were naturally suspect and couldn't seem to keep themselves from interrogating their loved ones.

"Why don't we work on that birdhouse we started?" he asked Ellie.

Ellie clapped her hands. "Yes! Is it time to paint it yet?"

"Almost. We have a few more sides to put on," he advised.

I shook my head. "You're building a bird mansion. That thing has more holes than the Welsh mansion has doors. You're going to have twenty birds living in there."

They both laughed as they walked through the door that led into the garage. I pulled open the fridge and dug around for something I could throw together. I found a pound of hamburger and a can of spaghetti sauce in the pantry. Spaghetti and meatballs, it was.

I tossed the ingredients into a bowl and began mixing, my mind going back to the moment I had opened the door to find Jacob standing there. It had been one of those moments where a person wasn't entirely sure they were seeing reality. It was his eyes. That's what told me I was looking at the bad boy I used to know. He was a man now, all grown up.

I stirred the meat into the eggs and seasoning before dropping the fork and going after it with my hands. I remembered the first time I had seen him in school. He'd been a junior and I a freshman. Jacob had quite the reputation as a bit of a troublemaker. It only made him all the more attractive to me. I loved his cocky smile and his carefree attitude. He didn't care that some people, including my father, thought he was a pain in the ass kid headed for a lifetime of lawbreaking. I think he secretly thrived on it. He loved to shake things up.

"And boy did he," I whispered.

I had finally caught his eye toward the end of my sophomore year and his senior year. The romance had been forbidden, making it all the hotter. We snuck off together every chance we got. I always found a way to get away from my father's watchful eye until the one night he decided to check up on me at my friend's house. I wasn't there. I had never been there. She'd tried to cover for me, but the damage was done. I was busted and ended up grounded for the whole damn summer. Despite that, I managed to sneak out my bedroom window and rendezvous with Jacob. We managed to carry on together for nearly two years and then one day—he was gone.

I suspected it was because of my brother and father, but that didn't lessen the sting. He up and left town without a goodbye or a forwarding address. Nothing. He could have stayed. He could have fought for me. He could have asked me to run away with him. He didn't. He gave up as if I weren't worth the effort. It wasn't long after that I learned I was pregnant.

Part of me kept waiting and hoping he would come back, ready to fight for us. I gave birth and there was still no sign of Jacob. He'd left me and our child. I had to conclude he didn't feel the same for me as I felt for him. I had been madly in love with him and he didn't love me. I had been a foolish, young girl with a crush. He'd been a boy who'd been having fun. I squeezed my eyes shut. The hurt and anger was still very real.

I couldn't believe he was back. And Ivy had called him Larry's VP. What the hell was that all about? Certainly, that didn't mean he was staying in town? I couldn't deal with him in my life again. No—I couldn't deal with him leaving again. I had to keep my distance. All those old feelings had come bubbling up, blooming like a flower that hadn't seen the sun in days. I would not let him hurt me again. I would not let myself be foolish again.

I tossed the meatballs into the oven and headed out to the garage to check out the birdhouse situation. "It looks awesome!" I exclaimed, checking out the massive bird complex sitting on my father's workbench.

"I'm going to paint it pink and purple!" Ellie exclaimed.

I looked at my father, his face twisted in a grimace. "Yep, pink and purple."

I burst into laughter; loving that he was willing to indulge my daughter's wishes. "I think it will look fabulous. Maybe you could use that sparkly paint we saw at the craft store."

My dad groaned. Ellie clapped and jumped up and down. "Yes! Can we, Grandpa?"

He looked at me, shaking his head before turning to Ellie with a bright smile. "You bet, Pumpkin."

It might have been a little mean to suggest the sparkly paint, but after seeing Jacob and feeling all the old hurts, I was feeling a little angry with my father. A sparkling pink birdhouse in his front yard seemed like a fair bit of revenge.

"Ten minutes for dinner," I told them before heading back inside to set the table.

We sat down to our dinner of spaghetti and meatballs with some sliced bread. I listened as Ellie carried on about the treehouse she wanted my dad to build her for when she came to visit. He of course was going to indulge her every wish and promised to get started on it right away.

"Can I go swing?" Ellie asked after dinner.

"Yes," I answered, carrying empty plates to the sink.

I watched her through the window that overlooked the backyard. She climbed on the tire swing I had spent hours on when I was a little girl. She looked like Jacob in some ways and me in others. Just then, with her long hair flying behind her as she swung, I felt she looked like me. When she was frustrated or angry, she looked like Jacob. She had his hazel eyes that changed with her mood.

"Want to tell my why you're really here?" my dad asked, coming to stand next to me at the sink.

"What do you mean? I thought we'd stop by for a visit," I replied.

He chuckled. "Sure. I can see you're upset about something. Let's leave these dishes and have a seat."

It wasn't necessarily a request. I dropped the towel and took a seat at the small table. "Jacob's back," I blurted out.

I expected him to get angry, rage, yell, and make threats. He didn't. He let out a sigh as if he had expected it. "I see."

I waited for him to say more. When he didn't, I told him about our encounter at the mansion. "I don't know if he's back to say or if it was just dinner."

"Are you going to tell him about Ellie?" he asked in a quiet voice.

"I don't know. I didn't think I would ever have to tell him. It's been *eight* years," I said, still in disbelief.

"If he's here to stay, to work at that new place, he's bound to see Ellie or hear about her from folks around town. She isn't exactly a secret," he reminded me.

"I know. I just can't imagine what he'll say and do when he finds out about her. I'm not sure I'm ready for that."

He chuckled. "Honey, I don't think you get to be ready. He's here. She's here. He's going to find out. I think it would be wise to head off the disaster by being honest. You don't owe him anything, but I think it's only fair he knows the truth about that little girl. And he should hear it from you."

I stared at him. "Have you been abducted and replaced by pod people?" I questioned.

He grinned. "No."

"What made you change your mind about Jacob? You hated him," I reminded him.

He shrugged. "You guys aren't kids anymore. You made an adult choice, and you've really stepped up. Ellie is a wonderful girl. You've done a great job raising her. I think it's up to Jacob to decide if he wants to be a part of her life. Honestly, I've been feeling guilty these past few years, knowing I had a hand in her not knowing her father. I'd like to see her get that chance. If he doesn't want to be a part of her life, then I will personally run his ass out of town again. If he does, then I think you should encourage that. Ellie and Jacob both have a right to know," he lectured.

I mulled over his words. "I'll think about it."

"Do. I know it can't be easy, but think of your daughter and what *she* needs," he said in a soft tone.

"I will. I'm going to head out. I need to get her home and in the tub," I said, getting up from the table.

I called her from the backyard before we said our goodbyes and made our way back out the mansion. I didn't see the big truck in the driveway and hoped that meant Jacob was gone. I parked the car in the garage and quickly ushered Ellie upstairs, afraid he would appear out of nowhere again.

My dad had left me with a lot to think about, but before I told Jacob anything, I wanted to know what he was doing in Burning Butte and how long he planned on staying.

# 5

## JACOB

I looked at the plan Larry had given me. I was seated in his office on one of the luxury couches with him directly across from me on the other. He'd had a coffee service brought in, and we were sipping our morning coffee and going over his plans for the future. It was definitely an energetic goal—one I wasn't quite so sure would work.

I cleared my throat, trying to find the best way to tell him his plans were not likely to be welcomed with open arms. "This is great, Larry, really great. However, I think you might find the resistance to these changes to be formidable."

He scowled, looking down at his plans. "This area is ready to be developed. I think I can make Western Energies here in Burning Butte a huge success. The growth potential is amazing."

I nodded, agreeing with him but not sure others would see it that way. "The people that live here in Burning Butte have been around a long time. They like things a certain way and will fight tooth and nail against any kind of change, especially the kinds of changes you want to make."

"I'm going to be giving them jobs and bring business back to town; help boost the economy here. How could anyone be opposed to that?" he questioned.

I shrugged. "I didn't say it makes sense. It's just the way things are."

"We have the technology to get to those oil deposits around the area. That is going to be good for business. We'll need workers. They'll move here and need housing and places to shop. The construction industry around these parts will get a huge boost as will the shops and restaurants in town. Hell, the schools could use the influx of tax money as well. My company would donate a great deal of money to the schools, or build parks, whatever it takes to help ease our way in," he said in that smooth business tone of his. "No one could possibly be upset by that."

I smirked. "You wouldn't think, but there are some old-timers who are very set in their ways."

"Fine. We'll need a good PR campaign to help ease the way for us then. We'll create some brochures and hold a town hall of sorts. I want people around here to see I only mean to help and won't do anything that would be detrimental to this beautiful land," he said, nodding his head as he embraced the idea.

"That is a great idea," I agreed.

"Good, because you're just the man to head it up."

I blinked. "What? PR? I don't do PR," I said, shaking my head.

"You're the perfect man for the job. It won't be like PR. It will be you reconnecting with the folks you grew up with," he said with a bright smile. "They are more likely to trust you than a guy like me. I'm an outsider."

I slowly shook my head. "I don't think there are too many people around here that want to reconnect with me. I didn't leave a lot of friends behind. I was a bit of a hellion and made more than a few enemies."

He waved a hand. "That's history. People expect young men to be wild. That's part of growing up. I doubt they're going to hold any of that stuff against you."

I wasn't quite so sure about that. "I'll do what I can, but I'm making no promises. I want this to work. I want you to be successful, because if you are, I am." I winked.

He chuckled. "And you know you will be rewarded. This is a big deal. We can do this."

"I'll give it my best shot, but I'm warning you, the people around here have long memories. I doubt any of them have forgotten some of my antics, and I seriously doubt there are many that are willing to forgive."

"We'll figure it out," he said confidently.

"Thanks for inviting me to dinner the other night. Your home is beautiful. I think I might like to own something like that one day. Maybe not as big, but I like the privacy you have out there," I told him.

"Thank you. I don't think I could have gotten Ivy to move out here if I wouldn't have found something up to her very high, spoiled expectations. You can't take a girl out of her mansion and expect her to live in anything but something equally as spacious," he joked.

"I suppose not," I agreed, not really having any idea what that would be like. "You guys got lucky and found a nanny pretty fast."

He nodded. "We did. Ivy put an ad in the classifieds before we ever moved here. I have to admit I didn't have much hope of finding anyone that would fit what we were looking for, but Erin was perfect. The kids love her. Ivy loves her and she does an excellent job," he said.

"She's a good person."

"You two know each other?" Jacob asked.

"Used to. That was a long time ago," I said, thinking back to the days I had been able to hold her. I was never able to call her my girlfriend, but we both knew that's what we were to each other. We were boyfriend and girlfriend when it was just the two of us.

"Ha! I bet you two were a little more than friends, huh?" he said, bouncing his bushy eyebrows up and down. "She's quite the looker."

I smiled, trying to hide my irritation over the way he was talking about Erin. "Yes, she was and is an attractive woman."

"I don't understand how a woman like that is still single," Larry said, shaking his head. "Maybe she's just a little too good for the guys around here."

"Maybe."

"Maybe you're just the man she needs to sweep her off her

feet. She's a hell of a cook and great with the kids. She'd make any man a good wife," he said.

"It *is* interesting that she's still single," I murmured aloud.

"Are you interested? Maybe I could set the two of you up?" he offered.

I chuckled. "No, thanks. I don't need my boss setting me up on dates and certainly not with the nanny. Things might get a little weird."

"Nonsense. I want you to be happy, and I can't say I've spent a lot of time in town, but I didn't see a lot of young women that would catch your eye, if you know what I mean," he teased.

"I don't doubt that," I mumbled.

None of them would catch my eye because there was only one woman I wanted. She was the only woman who had managed to make me feel anything. I had dated other women, but none of them did anything for me. It was always her lips I felt, her satiny smooth skin under my hands. Erin was the woman I thought about when I closed my eyes or when I was taking a long drive down a lonely highway. It was thoughts of her and our time together that I always reverted to when I had some alone time.

No other woman could make me feel like she did. Her dad had been convinced it was a teenage infatuation that would pass. Her brother was convinced it was wrong and dirty to want a woman as much as I wanted his little sister. He couldn't possibly understand what I felt for her. She was the one for me. I hoped there was a chance she felt the same about me. If there was a chance, even the tiniest little ember burning in her heart for me, I intended to fan the flames and make her love me again.

Her brother and father could kiss my ass. I wasn't going to let them tell me who I could and couldn't love. I loved her and they could either accept it or move on. If she was the one who told me to get lost and made it clear there was nothing between us, I would leave her alone, but I didn't think that was going to happen. I had seen the way she looked at me. I had seen that flash of desire before Ivy had come in and interrupted us.

"Are you okay?" Larry asked.

I looked at him, snapping myself back to the present. "Yes, sorry, I was thinking about how I was going to go about making the townspeople like not only you and the company, but me. I'm wondering if drugging the water supply is an option?" I joked.

He laughed. "Where there's a will, there's a way."

"I'll keep that in mind. I'm going to head back to my office and reach out to a few guys I used to play football with. Maybe one of them will have a suggestion," I said, getting to my feet.

"Thank you for your hard work on this. Once we get our foot in the door, the rest will be just fine. It's going to take some rubbing elbows and kissing babies, but we'll get it done. With your charm and my good looks, no one can deny us," he said before bursting into laughter.

I groaned. "I hope you're right. If not, we'll be run out of town." I closed the door behind me. "Again," I said under my breath.

Larry didn't know the whole story about why I left Burning Butte, and I didn't plan on telling him. However, that didn't mean someone else wouldn't take it upon themselves to fill him in on the gossip. I didn't think it would bother Larry any considering he knew the man I was now, which wasn't anything like the young kid I had been. Minus my thing for Erin. I walked back to my office and grabbed a good old-fashioned pen and paper to start jotting down ideas about how I could win over the town. I tapped my pen on the yellow pad, waiting for inspiration to strike. Nothing was coming to mind—at least nothing that had anything to do with what I was supposed to be thinking about. I couldn't stop picturing Erin standing there in the doorway.

She'd been wearing a simple pair of worn jeans, a pair of ankle booties, and a loose, flowing shirt that was perfectly feminine and so her. Her figure had been a little shapelier, more womanly, but it was the same old Erin that filled my dreams. I longed to touch her, taste her.

"Fuck," I groaned. The familiar ache low in my belly combined with the permanent set of blue balls I'd had for years was very uncomfortable.

I pushed thoughts of Erin to the back of my mind where they always lingered and focused on getting on the good side of the mayor and the other old-timers that could make or break our venture here in Burning Butte.

# 6

## ERIN

It had been a full two weeks since I had seen Jacob. Part of me was hoping he had disappeared into the ether again. Another part of me longed to see him. Apparently, I had been distracted and "frazzled" according to Ivy, who insisted I take the night off. She asked if Ellie could have a sleepover with Mackenzie. Initially, I declined the offer, but then she used some dirty-handed tactics and had the girls ask me. I couldn't refuse two of the cutest little girls in the world.

I used the private stairs into the mansion and followed the sound of laughter until I found the kids in the huge playroom, bouncing around in the ball pit that had been installed. I loved that Ellie got a chance to play like a rich kid, but I made sure she understood we were not wealthy, and I would never be able to afford such luxuries.

"Okay, guys, I'm out of here!" I said, shouting over their squeals.

Ivy was in the corner, her earbuds plugged into her ears and a book in her hand. I waved to get her attention. She pulled out her headphones and smiled. "Sorry, I can watch them, but the noise makes me crazy. I would never make a good nanny," she said with a laugh.

"Are you sure you want to do this?" I asked her again.

"I'm absolutely positive. I need to spend some time with the kids. We're going to make s'mores later over the firepit," she announced.

"That will make them happy—and wired," I warned.

"I plan on letting them bounce until they are so tired, they can't walk. The s'mores will give them a short burst of energy, and then they will be out like lights," she assured me.

"Good luck with that. I'll have my phone on me. Call if you need anything."

"No problem. The driver is waiting to take you into town," she said.

"I can drive," I insisted.

"No. You're going out to have fun and unwind. I don't want you to worry about not drinking because you drove. Just give him a call when you're ready to call it a night. Unless you want to call it a morning," she said with a wink.

"No way. No, no, no," I said, denying the insinuation I would hook up with someone.

"Have some fun! You're young and single and the hottest girl in town. Use that to your advantage."

I laughed, walking out the door. Ivy was always telling me

to enjoy my youth before I got suckered into marriage and had no fun at all. In my opinion, marriage was supposed to be fun, the kind of fun where a person didn't need to go out to the bars. Ivy wasn't adjusting to the move very well. I hoped she and Larry could find a way to reconnect and soon. They were a good couple, but things were certainly strained.

I stopped to check my reflection in the large mirror that hung inside the foyer. I wasn't necessarily trying to impress anyone, but I wanted to look a step above my usual nanny/mommy look with no makeup and my hair tossed up on my head. I used the tip of my index finger to wipe away a tiny mascara smudge before heading out the door.

The black SUV was waiting in the driveway. I felt ridiculous being chauffeured, but Ivy wasn't the kind of woman who took no for an answer. I got in the back seat and told Damon, our usual driver when I had the kids with me, that I wanted to go to the Old Flame Saloon. He smiled and nodded, putting the vehicle in drive and winding around the huge circular driveway. I leaned back, looking forward to what I hoped was a relaxing night.

I walked into the saloon and headed directly for the long bar, taking a seat on a stool at the end before slapping my hand on the counter. "Hey, lady!" I called out.

My best friend, Marianne Wilson, turned around, the soda hose in her hand, prepared to shoot me with water. "You are so obnoxious," she said with a laugh.

"You know you've missed me."

"The only time I see you is when your ass is planted there. I didn't think you would actually show up," she said, making me my favorite rum and Coke drink.

I shrugged. "It's the only time I get to talk to you, and where else am I going to go on my night off? You're it."

"Thanks, I feel loved," she grumbled, sliding my usual drink toward me on a coaster.

"I'm good," I said, pushing it back.

"I can see how good you are. You need a drink judging by the luggage under those eyes. All the makeup in the world isn't going to hide those worry lines," she said with a knowing look.

I took the drink, sipping from the straw and shaking my head. "It's been a hell of a week."

"Kids driving you nuts? I knew the honeymoon period would wear off and the little terrors would get the best of you."

I gave her a look. "No. It isn't the kids. It's Jacob."

She frowned. "Jacob? I haven't heard that name in a long time. What's up with him?"

"He's back."

Her mouth dropped open. "No shit!"

I nodded. "Yep. He showed up to dinner at the Welsh house. From what I've gathered, he works for Mr. Welsh at Western Energies. I think I overheard him call him the vice president," I revealed, actually enjoying the gossiping.

"No way," she said, shock covering her face.

I smiled and nodded, actually kind of proud of him for making something of himself. "I guess he proved everyone wrong, huh?"

She giggled. "I suppose he did. Does your dad know? Philip?"

"My dad knows, but I'm not sure if Philip does. And, get this, my dad isn't even bothered by it. I think he was a little relieved to know he was back."

Her shock turned to confusion. "What? Why?"

"I don't know. I think he is feeling a little guilty about giving us such a hard time. He thinks I have to tell him about Ellie," I added.

She slowly nodded her head. "You do."

"No!" I protested, expecting her to side with me.

She raised an eyebrow, folding her arms across her chest. "He's going to find out."

"Maybe. He might have already gone back to wherever he's been for eight damn years," I snapped.

"You know how people talk around here. It's only a matter of time."

I sighed. "I know and I swear I'm not not telling him to be spiteful, but I want to know what kind of man he is. What if he's married? His wife might not be happy to know he fathered a kid. Hell, he could have other kids. I want to know who he is now."

"Erin, he's Ellie's dad," she reminded me.

"I know, I know, and I've always said I would tell her who he was one day, but what if he finds out he's a father and runs scared? I can't do that to her. If he isn't in a place where he can be in her life or if he doesn't want to be in her life, I'm not going to bother telling her," I said firmly.

"I can understand that, but how long do you think it's going to take you to find out what he's up to?" she asked.

I shrugged. "I don't know. I don't want to come right out and ask Larry. I got the feeling they were pretty good buddies. I'm not going to risk my job by saying anything bad about Jacob to him."

"If he is going to be living and working here, he's bound to talk to some of the people we went to school with. Everyone knew you two had a thing. It was the worst-kept secret. Everyone also figures he's Ellie's father despite you trying to say he wasn't. Wouldn't you rather be the one to tell him than idle gossip spilling the secret?" she asked.

I curled my lip, not liking my choices. "I'm supposed to be here having a drink and unwinding. You are only stressing me out more. You're a shitty bartender. I thought you were supposed to help solve my problems," I complained.

She snapped her bar towel at me. "I am, you just don't like my answers. Sit tight while I get those guys a couple beers."

I nodded, sipping the drink and thinking about what she had said. Jacob was somewhere in town; I just knew it. I knew Western Energies was gearing up for something big. Larry had been talking about bringing some of his people to town to get things off the ground. Jacob was one of his people. I still couldn't believe we both worked for the same guy. It was one of those freak coincidences that couldn't be explained.

Marianne returned, leaning her elbows on the bar. "Is he still good-looking?" she asked.

I grinned. "Yes, he is, damn him."

She burst into laughter. "Did he see Ellie?"

"No. I'm not sure how I'm going to keep him from putting two and two together if he does see her. She looks enough like him that he would be able to figure out without me telling him," I said, dreading that moment.

"You're right, which is why you need to find him and let him know up front. This gives you the chance to lay some ground rules. Ellie never has to know. You and Jacob discuss the situation, and then figure out where to go from there. That's the adult way to handle this," she lectured.

I rolled my eyes. "There's the bartender we'd been missing."

She winked. "I give great advice. You may not like it, but it's good."

"Ugh. I was prepared for this moment for years, and then when it never happened, I just assumed it never would. He's known where to find me. If he wanted to see me again, he could have come back. He didn't, which makes me think he's moved on and has no room in his life for a kid," I said, almost convincing myself that was the case.

Deep down, I knew the Jacob I had known all those years ago would demand to be a part of his child's life. He would be pissed to know he'd missed out on so much time. His home life wasn't good. We had talked about our future together and how we would raise our children. I sighed, thinking back to those days of sitting on the ridge under the stars after we'd made love and talking for hours. We shared everything. I knew him better than anyone else, and he knew me better than even Marianne. Then one day he was gone. I had felt like I had lost a piece of my soul when I figured out he wasn't coming back. "I need another drink," I muttered, quickly downing the first one.

Marianne smiled. "I know you do."

She quickly poured me another before sliding it over to me. "Thanks."

"It's going to be okay. No matter how this goes, you have Ellie, you have me, and you have your family. Best-case scenario, he apologizes for abandoning you and the two of you get back together and raise Ellie. Worst case, he turns tail and runs away—again."

I shook my head. "Your worst case might very well be the best case depending on what kind of man he is."

I thought about her idea of best case. It was dangerous to let myself think that was even a possibility. I couldn't deal with the heartbreak all over if he walked out on me again. I would kill him if he did it to Ellie. My baby girl deserved a loving father that would never dare leave her. Before I told Jacob anything, I was going to put some of my father's interrogation techniques to use. I was going to interview Jacob and see if he was worthy of meeting my little girl. I was the one who'd taken care of her for eight years, staying up long nights and dealing with the puke and the poopy diapers and all the tears—she was mine.

# 7

JACOB

I wasn't getting far with my plans to infiltrate the town gossip ring to find out what was being said about Western Energies. Most of the people I remembered were not keen to talk to me. How could they possibly dislike me more? I hadn't been around to do anything to warrant their irritation.

I decided to try a different route. Alcohol was one of the best ways to get people to loosen up. It also tended to unleash some tempers as well, but I was hoping for the first. I needed to see what the local buzz was about our company. Once I knew what I was up against, I could come up with a good plan of attack.

The local bar was *the* place to be. It was where all the old-timers hung out, and then it was the people my age. That was where I would be able to take the temperature of the town. I could also really use an ice-cold beer. I was looking forward to walking into a place that I could be completely casual. It was one of the things I missed the most about my hometown—just being completely relaxed. No one was going to be looking at my clothes to try and determine if they were designer. I could just be old Jacob and drink beer straight from the bottle.

I parked my truck in the gravel parking lot, smirking at the very fact it was still gravel. I pushed open the door and was immediately transported back several decades. The Old Flame Saloon had not changed much over the years. It still smelled like stale beer, and the scent of cigarette smoke from way back when still clung to the walls. It was dark and dingy with only the muted bar lights with a few of the neon signs lit up to provide light. I looked around and spotted the pool tables in the back with the ugly-ass green lights hanging over them.

My eyes scanned the room, noticing there was a good-size crowd with a combination of young and old. I looked toward the bar and froze. I would know her anywhere. Her hair was loose and hanging down her back. I didn't even stop to think about what I was going to do; I just found myself taking long strides to get there.

"We need to talk," I said firmly, bending down and speaking directly into her ear.

Erin's head whipped around, her eyes going wide as she looked up at me. "Um, Jacob. What are you doing here?" she stammered.

"I want to talk with you."

"I don't think that's a good idea," she said, shaking her head before taking a sip from her drink.

"Erin, I'm sorry it's been so long," I told her.

Her eyes widened with surprise all over again. "You're sorry?"

I scowled, wondering why that was such a surprise. I wasn't that much of a dick. "Yes. Can we please go somewhere quiet and talk?"

She shook her head. "I have one night off, and about the last thing I want to do is go to a quiet place and talk."

I raised my hand to order myself that cold beer I'd been craving. The male bartender quickly delivered. I dropped a ten-dollar bill and told him to keep the change. Greasing the wheels included fat tips. With my beer in one hand, I reached down and grabbed her drink from her hand and walked to a quiet booth on the opposite side of the bar from the pool tables.

"Hey!" Erin protested.

I turned and held up her drink, smiling and inviting her to come and get it. She glared at me but slid off the stool and followed. I needed her to know I was still the guy she had loved all those years ago. She sat down opposite me and snatched her drink, taking a long drink. I watched her pretty red lips wrap around the straw before looking into those dark eyes that could entrance a man. "I've missed you," I blurted out.

She blinked. "What?"

"There isn't a day that goes by that I don't think about you. I've missed you," I said again.

I knew it was bold and very much directly to the point, but I had been thinking about the reunion with her for a long time. I had told myself if I ever got the chance to see her again, I would tell her how much I missed her. I wasn't going to play games or try and act like a tough guy. I had done that once, and it had cost me her. I needed her to know I was serious.

"Really? You've missed me, but you've known exactly where I was all this time and you never once came back? I don't know if I believe you," she said.

I shook my head. "It wasn't quite so cut-and-dry. I can admit I should have pushed back when they ran me out of town."

"What? Who?"

I raised an eyebrow. "Your brother. Your dad. They made it very clear I would not be welcome anywhere. They were both going to use their considerable influence to keep me from being able to get a job, an apartment, anything. I knew they were serious."

She looked at me, and I could see the hurt in her eyes. "I knew they wanted you to stay away from me, but I had no idea they had gone so far as to threaten your future here."

I nodded. "I'm sorry. I know I should have tried harder, but truthfully, they intimidated me. I didn't know how I would live or support myself if they followed through with their threats, which I believe they absolutely would have."

"I didn't know," she said in a soft voice.

"It was a long time ago. I've done a lot of growing up, and those threats don't mean shit to me now," I said, fighting back the anger that came with the memory of those times.

"I wasn't thrilled to know they had interfered, but that was a long time ago. Things have changed," she said nonchalantly.

I reached out and grabbed her hand. "Have they changed that much? I have never stopped thinking about you. I'm back. I'm living here, and I want to see if we can make things work again."

Her mouth fell open. "Jacob, that was a long time ago."

"So? I never stopped caring about you. Never. Eight years and you are still the only woman I want," I said.

I knew I was putting myself out there and giving her the full capability to shatter my heart, but I didn't care. I would recover. I had been waiting for the moment I could have her back in my life for too damn long to worry about my feelings getting hurt or feeling vulnerable. She was worth it.

She tried to pull her hand away from mine. I didn't let her. Her eyes searched mine. "Jacob, there is so much time, so much... everything."

I nodded. I could feel her hand trembling in mine. "I know there is a lot. We've changed. We've grown up, but that doesn't mean our feelings for each other are gone. I know it's still there for me. I worked my ass off to get to a point where I could come back and prove to your family I was worthy of you. I know I didn't make a great impression back then. I know I screwed up a lot and I made some pretty shitty decisions, but I've changed. I'm not that same stupid kid."

She was looking at me with such hope and wonder, but I could see she wasn't sold. "What if what you're feeling is nothing more than memories?"

"It's more than that."

"How do you know?"

"Because I look at you right here, right now, and it all comes flooding back. It's like no time has passed. I want to see if we can rekindle that flame that once burned so bright. You know how good it was. I know you felt the same way about me," I told her, not willing to accept anything other than the truth.

She looked away, not pulling her hand from mine but using her free hand to pull her drink closer. I could feel the turmoil running through her. I knew I had surprised her by coming back and again by telling her I wanted to be with her.

"Are you seeing anyone?" I asked.

I didn't care if she was. I would fight the dude if I had to. I was not going to walk away so easily this time.

She slowly shook her head. "No. You?"

"No."

"Have you ever been married? Long-term relationship?" she questioned.

"I have not been married, not even close. I've not been in any real relationship since you. You?" I asked, almost afraid to hear the answer.

I didn't want to think about her with another man. I didn't want to think about her telling another man she loved them. I knew I didn't have any claim to her the eight years I had been gone, but I sure as hell didn't want to think about it or know for certain.

"No, I've been too busy for that," she said with a wave of her hand.

I didn't know what that meant. She'd been in Burning Butte. How busy could she have been?

"Good," I said, not afraid to let her know I still considered her mine.

She finished off her drink but lifted her hand to get the attention of one of the barmaids. I was surprised to see her drinking so fast but imagined seeing me and talking to me about a relationship was a lot to take in.

"Jacob, thank you for the apology, but this, this thing between us, is really a bad idea. I don't think I can go down that road again," she said.

I felt like she had stabbed me in the heart. I had hoped and prayed and hoped some more that she would give me a chance if I was completely honest with her. I had put it all out on the line, and she was going to shoot me down. I couldn't accept defeat. Not that easy. I wasn't going to give up.

"Erin, I'm not going away. I'm buying a house in town. I'm here to stay. You're going to be seeing a lot more of me. I'm serious when I tell you I want to get to know you all over again. I'm not talking shit or saying nice things. I'm dead serious," I said, staring directly into her eyes.

8

ERIN

I wasn't drunk—not drunk enough to think starting up with Jacob was a good idea. However, I was just buzzed enough to let myself think about the good ol' days. They had been good. They had been glorious days, but I wasn't naïve enough to think I could go back to them. The past was the past, and no matter how hard a person tried, there was no return.

Despite knowing it was a horrible idea, I couldn't quite dismiss the idea of him entirely. His strong hand over mine was making me a little crazy. There was the slightest hint of danger that drew me in. I knew what people would say if they heard we were together again after all this time. I knew they would talk and whisper. There was something about Jacob that was impossible to resist.

"Why are you back here?" I asked him.

I had heard the rumors, heard the frustrated gossip from those around town that weren't pleased to have Larry

Welsh and his company in the area. "Larry offered me a job that was too good to pass up," he answered smoothly.

"But why here? Why are you here in Burning Butte of all places? I know he has offices all around the country," I said.

He smiled. "Because you're here. I had unfinished business with you."

I shook my head. "I think there is some kind of statute of limitations on old relationships. You can't show up out of the blue, nearly a damn decade later, without any kind of contact in all that time and expect things to go back to the way they were. That ship sailed when you hightailed it out of town without a word."

He continued holding my hand, using his free hand to take a long drink from his beer bottle. "I already told you, that wasn't my choice. I wanted to stay. I wanted to come back many times before, but I knew it would only result in more of the same. I didn't want to put you in the middle of a fight between me and your family. I know you love them, and I would never make you choose. I had to go away and make something of myself so I could come back and prove to your dad and brother I was worthy of you."

"What have you been doing these past eight years?" I asked.

He let out a long breath. "After I left here, I kind of stumbled around a bit. I ended up in Washington. I went to college and got my bachelor's degree."

"You did? How?" I asked, somewhat skeptical.

I knew he'd been poor. His family didn't have any money. How in the hell had he managed to pay for it?

He chuckled. "I worked three jobs and have a shit ton of student loan debt, but I made it work."

I was thoroughly impressed. That had to have taken some serious determination. I knew how hard it was to go part-time.

"I was determined to come back. When I started with Larry, he'd talked about the Dakotas. When he offered me the job with a position here in Burning Butte, it was like fate finally stepped in and gave me the opportunity I needed. I wasn't about to pass it up. I've always been intent on coming back to reclaim what I was forced to leave behind," he said, his voice rolling over me and leaving my skin feeling tingly.

I licked my lips, trying my hardest not to look at his mouth, but it was futile. I couldn't stop staring at his lips and wondering what it would be like to kiss him again.

"Good for you," I murmured for lack of anything better to say.

"Erin, why don't we go somewhere where we can have this conversation in private, without half the town eavesdropping?" he asked, leaning forward.

I looked around and noticed there were more than a dozen eyes on us. We were making quite the scene. It wouldn't be long before my dad was informed of our deep conversation.

"Okay," I whispered.

He got to his feet, letting go of my hand. I followed him out the door, ignoring the many looks in our direction. He pointed to a dark truck in the lot, using his key fob to unlock the doors. I climbed in and Jacob started the truck, and drove out of the parking lot, heading north. I knew exactly where he was going. It was our spot.

He turned off the road and followed the dirt road up to the butte on the northside of town. He parked, turned off the engine and turned to look at me. I stared at the lights of our small town stretched out below. It was always so much prettier up here than it was down below. The stars were brighter, and there seemed to be a million more than what could be seen from our backyards.

"Why didn't you call me? I tried calling you and you shut off your phone," I said, turning to face him in the dark cab of the truck.

"My phone was shut off because I couldn't pay the bill. I didn't call you because I had been warned against it. I didn't want you to get in any trouble. I promise you; I hadn't meant for it to take me so long to get back to you. I would have been back earlier if it were possible," he insisted.

I shook my head. "You just left me," I whispered, my voice breaking as I remembered the hurt I had felt.

He reached out and put his arm around me and pulled me closer to him. The damn seats made it difficult for any real cuddling, but I let myself go into his arms. His warmth and strength enveloped me, and I had to admit it felt nice.

"I'm sorry. I hated being away from you, but I couldn't come back before I was ready. If I had come back too soon, I wouldn't be strong enough to take on your dad and brother. Things would have gone badly, and I would have been forced out all over again." His voice was low and full of emotion.

I couldn't stop the tears from sliding down my cheeks. My heart had been broken. It had ached for years. I had gone through a period of doubting myself and wondering what was wrong with me that he left me without a word.

"You could have left a note or sent a text," I said.

He turned, his body facing mine looking into my eyes and the filtered moonlight streaming through the windshield. "I wanted to. My god, I wanted to, but there was no way they were ever going to let me have you," he said, using the pad of his thumb to wipe away the few tears that had streaked down my cheek.

My heart was doing a happy dance, pitter-pattering and making me feel all warm and tingly. His words were the balm I had been looking for. In that moment, I believed him. "Why now?"

"Because now was the right time. Now, I'm ready to fight to get you back. I've never stopped thinking of you or wanting you. I swear, my entire world has revolved around me getting back to you."

His sweet words were making me feel drunk with happiness and longing for him. His hand cupped my face as he stared into my eyes. My gaze dropped to his lips. He clearly took that as his cue to take what we'd both been longing for and brushed his lips over mine. I stiffened. It was like getting hit by a zap of electricity. I gasped, my lips parting just enough to give him the go-ahead to take the kiss to the next level.

His tongue slid into my mouth and we both moaned in unison. All the old feelings came flooding back with the contact. I scooted closer to him, needing to feel him against me. His hand moved through my hair, coming to rest on the back of my neck. His hot fingers were sending shivers of delight up and down my spine as his mouth worked over mine. It took no time at all for the kiss to go from tender and searching to hot and needy.

It was like no time had passed at all. I reached up to run my hand through his short hair, then slid it down his back and felt the corded muscles there. He was different and the same, and I wanted him. I started to feel desperate, like I couldn't get enough of him. He must have sensed my need. His hand moved down my body, stopping for a brief second to roughly massage my breasts before undoing the button on my jeans.

I pulled away from him, leaning back in the seat to pull my jeans down while he worked at his. I heard the quiet hum of his seat moving back and the bounce of the tilt steering wheel going up. I glanced over, saw his erection standing proud in the moonlight, and was encouraged to move faster. With my jeans off, I crawled over the center console and straddled him. My hands held his face. I looked into his eyes, angry with him for leaving me but so desperate to be with him. I wiggled my hips, finding the exact spot I needed, and slowly pushed my body down his.

His mouth was hot, his tongue dancing and dueling with mine as our bodies very slowly came together. It had been a long time. It took a few attempts to get things right, but the moment my body opened up for his invasion, I slid down over him. He groaned loudly next to my ear, his hands resting on my hips as I struggled to catch my breath. The intrusion felt good and right, and I needed a second for my body to adjust.

I moved against him, pulling away from him and leaning

against the steering wheel as I ground my hips against him. He hissed, sucking in air through his teeth. His hands moved under my shirt, pushing the bra up and touching my breasts. I moaned, dropping my head back, my nose practically rubbing over the roof of the cab as I let ecstasy lead the way. His hands were big and strong, just like the rest of his body. I reached one hand between us, pressing my palm against his chest and feeling the hard muscles.

"Oh god," I whispered, my body beginning to contract around his.

I couldn't stop it from happening. The man was deep inside me, tickling every nerve. Streaks of white-hot fire coursed through my body, making me jerk and spasm as I moved faster, chasing the release I had gotten a little glimpse of.

"Get it, baby," he whispered, his hand squeezing my breast, the other squeezing my ass and yanking me hard against him.

"Oh god," I cried out again, unable to stop the orgasm from washing over me with a strong tidal wave effect, pulling me under and completely surrounding me.

# 9

## JACOB

I held back for as long as I could, letting her set the pace, but I was quickly losing control. She felt so good, so right. It was as if my body recognized her and was just as eager to rekindle all those feelings that only she could give me. Her body was the one I craved, the one I longed for on lonely nights. Her sounds of ecstasy rang in my ears. There was no stopping my climax. I would have loved to drag it out, make it last all damn night, but my body had been starved for her for too long.

I felt her release, her body squeezing mine and pulling me deeper inside her. I shifted in the seat, trying to get deeper, wishing like hell we were in a bed where I could get some leverage. It didn't matter. I still found the ecstasy I was searching for.

"Shit," I breathed out as I was clutched in the tightest, sweetest vice.

I stiffened, unable to move or control my jerking hips as I found my release. I never thought it could ever be like that with her again. Part of me had begun to think I had made it up or embellished the fantasy of her. I knew that was all wrong now. It was that good. It was better than good. She collapsed against me, her head resting on my shoulder. I wrapped my arms around her, hugging her tight.

Neither of us talked for several long minutes. I could feel her heart beating against mine. It was soothing and made me think there was hope. How could two people come together like that and not *be* together? Our bodies were meant for one another. She'd been primed and ready with no effort from me. She wanted me. That thought filled me with so much joy I thought my heart would explode.

Just when I thought I would get a chance for round two, a flash of headlights washed over us. "Oh shit," she gasped, rolling off me and climbing into the passenger seat. She was yanking on her jeans, cursing under her breath. I quickly stuffed myself into my pants and had them zipped and buttoned when the car parked about twenty feet away. I imagined it was a couple looking for a little privacy.

"We should go," Erin mumbled, pulling on her shoes.

I adjusted my seat, fixed the steering wheel, and turned on the engine, then slowly drove back down the hill. Neither of us spoke. I was trying to think of the right thing to say. I had a fifty-fifty chance of sending her running in the opposite direction or getting another chance to be with her. I pulled into the parking lot, parking my truck close to the back edge, hoping we could get a chance to talk. She had her phone in her hand, furiously texting.

"Erin, I want to see you again," I said.

She sighed, putting her phone back in her pocket, and

turned to look at me. The look on her face was not what I had been hoping to see. The bit of hope I had after our brief interlude together vanished. "Jacob, what just happened, it doesn't change anything."

"I think it proves we both want each other," I replied.

"It was nice, but it can't happen again."

"Nice?" I said, raising my eyebrows. "Baby, that wasn't just nice," I said, watching her blush under the lights in the parking lot.

"Mind-blowing sex isn't exactly a relationship. It was good. Is that what you need to hear?" she asked somewhat irritably.

I grinned. "It doesn't hurt to hear that, but you know it's more than that. It's always more than that."

She slowly shook her head. "We were kids back then. We were young and crazy and had no real-life experience. We thought we had something special. It's called puppy love for a reason. We didn't know what it was like to be in a relationship with responsibilities and plenty of obstacles," she said.

"It wasn't puppy love. I know you felt the connection then, and I know you feel it now," I argued.

"No, I felt sex. That's what we shared just now," she retorted.

"Bullshit. I know you better than that," I said, not believing her for a second.

She turned to look out the window. "Jacob, we're different people. You don't know me anymore. It's been eight years. We've both grown and changed. We can't go back. Those days are gone. I know the idea of being together sounds appealing and it might feel like we can pick up where we left off, but the reality is, we can't. Too much has happened. Too many hurt feelings and just too much of everything," she said with frustration.

I reached out to touch her. She didn't pull away which I was taking as a good sign. "We're older and we've both changed —you're right. But we're more mature and that means were ready to deal with an adult relationship."

"Jacob, don't you ever wonder why we didn't go the distance before? I mean, yes, my family was difficult, but if we were really in love, we both would have fought harder. I wouldn't have had to keep us a secret, and you wouldn't have left. We were infatuated, and yes, we had great sex, but that doesn't mean anything in the grand scheme of things," she protested.

I shook my head. "No, don't say that. I wanted to go the distance. I'm here. I'm ready to do this. I want to make this a real thing. I'll stand up to anyone who tries to get in my way. Maybe I wasn't ready for the real thing back then, but I am now."

"It's not that easy, Jacob! You know nothing about me or my life, and I don't know anything about you!"

"You do know me, and I know you. Yes, I want you to fill in the blanks, but no matter what has happened, you're still the girl I knew back then. I could *feel* it," I stressed.

She sighed. "You felt a natural reaction to sex. That's all," she said and opened the door, jumping out before I got a chance to come up with a good response.

It was more than sex. I knew it and she knew it. She was being stubborn. She wasn't going to let me waltz back into her life without putting up a little resistance. It didn't surprise me at all. In fact, if she hadn't played a little hard to get, I'm not sure it would have been as interesting. I watched her get into the back of an SUV and recognized it as the same one Larry often used.

There was a knock on my driver's-side window, startling me. I turned to see Philip Maxwell standing there in his sheriff's uniform. I had heard he'd been voted in last year. I wasn't surprised. Like father, like son. Even when we were younger, he had said he was going to grow up and be the sheriff just like his dad. We had joked around I would be his deputy. Those were the days we were best friends, the days before his sister and I started seeing each other.

I hit the button for the window and let it slide down, both of us staring at each other. He had intimidated me once, but not anymore. Neither of us said a word as we glared at one another. I dared him to try and run me out of town. He didn't know who he was messing with now.

"Did I just see Erin climb out of here?" he asked in a tight voice.

I wasn't going to deny it. Part of me being back meant I was going to let the entire town know I was after Erin. I didn't give a shit what any of them thought.

"You did," I said defiantly.

Philip slowly shook his head. "You are one dumb son of a bitch, aren't you?"

"Actually, no, I'm not."

"I thought you would have learned before that Erin is off-limits. You don't get to see her or be with her," he growled. "We told you before, stay the hell away from her. She is too good for you."

I shrugged a shoulder. "Maybe she is, but she's a big girl and she can make her own decisions now."

"Not when it comes to you. I'm serious—stay away from her," he warned.

I smirked. "Are you her keeper? Are you going to throw her in jail if she talks to me? Are you going to throw me in jail? That's right, you like to intimidate and scare guys that don't know any better. News flash, *Sheriff*," I said with a sneer. "You don't intimidate me in the slightest. It will take a much bigger man than you to run me out of here now."

"I'm not joking, Jacob. Stay the hell away from her. She doesn't need your bullshit. Leave her alone," he hissed.

My smirk faded and I got very serious. "It isn't going to work this time. I'm not about to be intimidated by some small-town sheriff. I'll leave her alone when she tells me to do so, but Philip, fair warning, I don't think she's going to be telling me leave her alone," I said with a smile, unable to resist poking him just a little. He certainly fucking deserved it after the hell he'd put me through.

He glowered. "You sure about that?"

I nodded. "Positive. Whatever happens between me and Erin and I is none of your business. It wasn't your business back then either. I damn sure mean to make it a lot clearer this time. You won't interfere with my life a second time."

Philip looked like he had something to say about that, but I

65

didn't give him the chance. I put the truck in drive and hit the gas, forcing him to step back. I pulled out of the parking lot, being careful to use my blinker. I wasn't going to give him a reason to pull me over and give me a hard time. I wasn't going to be the troublemaker. He could try and fuck with me, but it wouldn't work. I knew my rights, and I was not about to let his podunk ass bully me.

He and his dad thought they were king shit because they wore badges. They could intimidate some people, but not me, not anymore. Now that I had a taste of Erin, I was hooked. I was ready to go the distance and make her realize I was back, and I intended on winning her heart. I drove out to the inn, my mind jumbled with a million different thoughts.

I needed to make her see she wanted me. I felt her want, her need. Now, I just needed to ease back into her life and prove to her I wouldn't run out and leave her high and dry again. Those days were gone. Once she agreed to be mine, she was going to be stuck with me. I parked the truck and headed inside the small room. I couldn't wait to get a house of my own. I had it in the works, but damn if the paperwork didn't take forever. I needed to settle in, show Erin what I could offer her, and make her see I was a man capable of taking care of her. I had gone out and done what I had to in order to give her that life we had dreamed about together. I could give her everything.

## 10

### ERIN

Friday night was on a constant repeat in my head. I couldn't turn it off. I kept replaying it all over and over, wondering what in the hell had gotten into me. I couldn't blame alcohol. I had two drinks. I wasn't stone-cold sober, but I wasn't drunk. He'd been on my mind since I had seen him that day. Then he touched me, comforted me, and I was lost. I wanted to know what it would be like to be with him one more time. My body craved his touch, and I was helpless to fight it any longer.

I shuddered at the memory of his kiss and the way he had felt inside me. It had been so much better than I remembered. Sex with a very adult Jacob was very different from sex with the younger version. Granted, we were still in the front seat of a truck, but there were some pretty big differences in the way he felt.

A happy squeal reminded me I was on duty. I was lounging on a chair in the backyard of the Welsh mansion with all three kids playing one of the giant yard games. They were going back and forth between the pool and the games set up on the lawn. We were taking it easy today and just hanging out, not worrying about math or running errands.

That left me with way too much time on my hands to think about Jacob. I wanted to believe he had changed. He seemed sincere, but I had never been able to resist his charms. Like that night in his truck. I still couldn't believe I had done that. I was the one who'd initiated the sex. I was the one to blame. I acted like there were no consequences when I knew better. I had thrown caution to the wind and mounted him without a care in the world.

I knew better. *Dammit!* My lack of caution back in high school could be explained by youthful immaturity. I didn't have the luxury of claiming that now. I couldn't help the smile that spread over my face as my mind traveled back to those days. I remembered the first time Philip brought Jacob home after school. I had been a typical teenage girl with a raging crush. I had flirted and made a complete ass out of myself, embarrassing Philip. My dad assured Philip it was just a phase and it would pass.

It didn't. That crooked little smile had turned me inside out. I remembered going to the lake and watching him and Philip swim. I also remembered the many times the two of them got in trouble together and Jacob apologizing to my dad for dragging Philip into one mess or another. I knew Philip was often the instigator, but Jacob always took the fall and my dad always believed their story.

It was that bad-boy side of Jacob that drew me in. He had a hint of danger to him that sparked my inner rebel. I had always been a good girl living under the thumb of my very strict father. When I turned eighteen, that crush I had on Jacob became a full-blown infatuation. We'd snuck a few kisses here and there, and we had spent countless hours together talking and just being together, but it had never gone any further.

Jacob had been insistent he couldn't date because a guy didn't date his best friend's little sister. I thought it was total bullshit. Who cared what Philip thought? I sure as hell didn't. I had a burning desire for Jacob, and I didn't give a shit about the consequences. I loved the idea of doing something rebellious. Dating my brother's friend, the guy my dad disliked and urged Philip to stay away from, was the perfect way to satisfy my need to buck the rules.

My dad was convinced Jacob was a born criminal on a path to prison. Once he and Philip graduated, my dad had less control over how much time Philip spent with Jacob, which worked out great for me because I was always with my big brother. I loved flirting with Jacob. I knew he was interested, and I very quickly learned the art of tease.

No matter how much I teased and propositioned him, Jacob always shot me down. I'd get a kiss or two, and then he would back off and tell me we couldn't. I was not the kind of girl who took no for an answer. When I turned eighteen, I had tried to convince him I was legal. He was still not having it. After I graduated high school, I managed to get him alone again. The kisses between us were a regular thing, but I wanted more. I could feel he wanted me as well, but the dude had been stalwart in his decision not to touch me.

And then that night happened.

*I got out of Marianne's car, walking over the bumpy ground in the general direction of the glow from the bonfire. Mari-*

anne grabbed my hand, giggling softly as we approached the party taking place out in an open field far away from the long reach of the sheriff.

"I bet all the college guys are going to be here," she tittered.

"I'm only looking for one in particular," I said with a laugh.

"Girl, let it go. You've practically thrown yourself at him, and he keeps shutting you down."

"No way. I have to have him," I said, determined to show Jacob I was mature enough to be with him.

Music filled the air, coming from the open door of someone's car. There were pickup trucks parked around the area, backed up close to the fire with the tailgates down. Young ladies and men were sitting on the truck tailgates, legs swinging as they drank from red Solo cups. I scanned the area, finding my target. There was a pretty blonde practically hanging off him. I stared at him until his eyes met mine. He said something to the girl, hopped off the tailgate, and walked around the fire toward me. Our gazes held.

"Good luck," Marianne whispered before moving off to get a cup from the keg.

"What are you doing here?" he asked, a frown on his face.

I shrugged. "I wanted to party."

"Your daddy is going to kill you."

"Not if he doesn't know." I smiled.

He shook his head. "How'd you escape the handcuffs?"

"I swallowed the key," I said with a wink.

"Well, you're here, I suppose you should make the most of it. Want a drink?" he asked.

"Sure."

He left, coming back a minute later with a cup of warm beer. I tried to drink it, but it had been putrid. "Want to take a walk?" he asked when one of the partygoers cranked up his stereo so loud it was impossible to hear anything else other than the music.

I nodded, letting him take my hand and lead me away from the loud laughter that mingled with the country music pouring out of the speakers of the truck. We stopped in an area that was quiet with a few tall trees providing a nice breakup from the party. We sat down on a huge rock, and I made my move. I kissed him, letting him know what it was I wanted.

"Erin, we can't," he protested.

"We can. There's no one around. I'm old enough. Philip never has to know," I told him.

"I don't want to piss him off," he protested, his lips hovering over mine.

"If you don't kiss me, I'm the one you should be worried about pissing off," I said, grabbing the back of his head and kissing him with an intensity that revealed exactly what I wanted.

He stopped resisting and one thing led to another—

"Mom!" Ellie shouted.

I blinked several times, looking directly at her. "What?"

"Can we go in the pool again?" she asked.

"Yes, go ahead." I waved a hand.

They all raced toward the pool, climbing in and happily splashing each other. I watched Ellie, thinking back to that night. I had thought I was having a little fun with Jacob. I did have fun, but I also ended up pregnant. Our secret romance wasn't a secret for long. People at the party had noticed us slipping off together and it got back to Philip.

Pissed wasn't the word I would have used to describe Philip's reaction to the news. When he had confronted me about it, I didn't deny it. I refused to deny how I felt for Jacob, which had been exactly the wrong thing to do. My rebellion had cost me far more than I could have ever imagined.

I didn't know it then, but I learned later my dad had threatened to have Jacob thrown in jail for the smallest infraction. Jacob's penchant for trouble meant it would only be a matter of time before my dad could bust him for something minor and turn it into something big enough to ruin his life. When they had confessed that they had told him to stay away from me, I didn't talk to them for weeks. I had been so pissed at them, I was planning on running away and never speaking to them again. But then I found out I was pregnant.

I was eighteen, alone and pregnant with no job and no means to support myself. Jacob had fallen off the face of the earth. I had never felt so completely alone in my life. I finally had to swallow my pride and confess my sins—all of them. My dad had been disappointed and more than a little angry, but he helped me. He took care of me and let me stay at home. He cursed Jacob, and Philip vowed to hunt him down and kill him. Eventually, once Ellie was born, things settled down. Jacob was never spoken of again.

I sighed, thinking about what he must have felt getting run out of town. He was back, and it was clear he was hell-bent on revenge. I didn't blame him. However, his idea that we could pick up where we left off and pretend like everything was okay wasn't ever going to work. He would find out about Ellie. I knew how he felt about Philip for what he'd done. Jacob wasn't the forgive-and-forget type. When he realized what I had been keeping from him, that anger would be turned on me.

How would he react? Would he hate me? Would he try and fight for custody? My stomach churned at the idea of Ellie being dragged into an ugly mess. What kind of revenge would he seek when he learned he had a daughter?

I rubbed a hand over my face. I was going to have to come up with a plan and fast. I was already on borrowed time. Someone in town would tell him about Ellie. Hell, Larry might even mention the fact I had a daughter. I was playing with fire. I either had to tell him or resort to drastic measures. I didn't know what those measures were but running away was the first thing that came to mind. I knew it would only make matters worse. One of my dad's favorite sayings was your sins will always find you out. That had been proven true time and again.

I did not want to be on the other end of Jacob's wrath if he had to chase me. I was going to have to bite the bullet and tell the man he had a daughter. I groaned, pushing the plan to a back burner for now. That was a lot easier said than actually done.

## 11

## JACOB

Thinking about anything other than Erin's lush body over mine was next to impossible. I knew I had work to do and that I was slightly obsessing, but that didn't stop me from reliving every second from the very moment we kissed until she collapsed against me, wet and spent in the front seat of my truck. I couldn't think about that right then. I had spent all weekend thinking about it. Now, it was time to figure out how to make Burning Butte welcome Western Energies. Maybe welcome was a strong word. If I could get them to simply allow us to do a job, they would see we weren't there to destroy their small town or make it into a sprawling metropolis.

There was a rap on my door before it was flung open. I looked up to see Larry, a scowl on his face as he closed the door behind him. It didn't look good. "Larry?" I said.

He sat down, looking very unhappy. "We've got a problem."

My stomach sank. Somehow, he'd found out about me and Erin and was going to warn me away from her. I couldn't do it. I wouldn't do it. Larry couldn't dictate my personal life. My mind was already working in overdrive, thinking about the many arguments I would put forth about why I could and would be with Erin.

"What problem would that be?" I asked, keeping my voice even.

"I just left a city council meeting," he grumbled, shaking his head. "You would have thought I walked into enemy territory. They are all going to block the expansion. They say there are some zoning laws that prohibit us from doing any kind of oil drilling out there in the middle of nowhere. I don't even think half of them knew the area I was speaking about!"

I sighed, expecting as much. "I warned you this would be an uphill battle."

"Uphill! They won't even let me get my damn foot in the door. I've already called my lawyer," he growled.

I winced. Suits and lawyers who wore them would go over with the city council about as well as a lead balloon. He was fighting the fight like he was in a city. Burning Butte did things a little differently. He needed to speak their language and acknowledge their angst over losing the way things had always been done. It was going to be one of those situations that required nice, thick, sweet honey to lure them. A pissy, vinegar-filled attitude was only going to make the situation worse.

"Larry, I think there is a better way," I started.

"There better be. My lawyer said this thing could be tied up in court for years. I'm not here to burn money. I'm here to make money. I can't afford to sit around paying a legal team and not bring in a profit," he complained.

I nodded. "I understand."

"I need real results," he reiterated.

"I get it."

"What's your plan to help the people around here understand this could be very good for them?" he asked, putting the problem squarely in my lap.

I grimaced, not really having any better ideas to offer. "I don't know. Yet. I'm working on it."

Larry shook his head. "This is a big deal for us."

"I know. I'm not giving up. I'm just looking for the right angle to go at this," I told him, not wanting him to think he'd wasted his time and energy hiring me.

"Maybe you were right. You've been gone too long, and the people here consider you an outsider."

"I told you I wasn't on great terms with a lot of the people around here. But that doesn't mean I can't find a way to make them like you, the company, and maybe even me," I said with a grin.

He looked me right in the eye, completely serious. "I don't think I have to tell you if this doesn't go through, there is no job for you. This job was created for you at Western Energies. If we can't drill, I'll need to sell this division. I can't guarantee the next owner will keep you on."

"I understand."

He rose to his feet and walked to the door, pausing to look back at me. "I encourage you to find a way in with these people sooner rather than later. If you have to suck up to the whole damn city council, do it. We need this."

I nodded. "I'm working on it."

He left me alone, the weight of the world on my shoulders. My entire goal in coming back to Burning Butte was to be successful. If I lost my job, I would only prove all of them right. They could laugh me right out of town a second time, and there was a damn good chance I would lose Erin for good.

I had to dig deep. There had to be common ground somewhere. Once I found it, I could promote. If there was something the town needed that Western Energies could provide, beyond the obvious jobs and influx of business to the various shops and restaurants barely getting by, I could use it. Western Energies had endless resources.

"What does Burning Butte want?" I murmured, tapping my pen on the pad.

I thought back to my days growing up here. What did I wish we had? I smirked, thinking back then I would have liked a sports bar or a nice place to play basketball with the guys. There was only one thing I wanted in Burning Butte now. Erin. Erin was what I wanted and needed.

I stopped tapping the pen. My needs might actually be the answer. If I could get Erin to accept me, there was a good chance she could speak to her family. With her dad the retired sheriff and her brother the acting sheriff, the Maxwell family was the key to unlocking the city council. With the Maxwell family on our side, I was confident we could get the zoning laws changed and Western Energies could begin operations.

I grimaced, thinking back to the last words Erin had said. She said we couldn't see each other again. However, the situation with Western Energies might actually work in my favor. Erin worked for Larry. If he sold the company, there was no reason for him to stay in town. He'd likely sell the mansion and move back to Dallas. I knew that's what his wife was angling for. There would be nothing to keep him or his family in the small town if he couldn't make any money. He was a wealthy man for a reason. He didn't sit around waiting for money to fall into his lap. He went out and found a way to make it. I knew she would likely give me some resistance, but I could be persuasive. I was looking forward to persuading her. At least it meant I would get the chance to see her again.

I grabbed my keys, wallet, and phone and headed out of the office without saying a word. Things were a little slow right now; I doubted anyone would miss me. I drove out to the Welsh mansion, hoping Erin would be working. With the kids out of school, there was a good chance she was home. I was going to pitch my idea of working together. I wasn't expecting it to be accepted right off, but I was hoping I could convince her it was a way for both of us to keep our jobs.

I rang the bell, looking forward to seeing Erin. It wasn't Erin's face I saw when the wide door opened, however. "Hi," I greeted Mrs. Welsh.

Her face broke into a huge smile. "Well, hello there, handsome. You're certainly a sight for sore eyes."

I chuckled. "Hello, Mrs. Welsh. You look beautiful, as always," I said with a wink.

A little innocent flirting always worked wonders for a woman's self-esteem. I didn't mind giving her a little boost. She seemed a little needy, the type that needed to be told she was beautiful—a lot.

She wrinkled her nose. "Call me Ivy. Mrs. Welsh is Larry's mom. I'm not that much older than you."

"Will do, *Ivy*," I said, stressing her name and keeping my smile in place.

"Does my husband know you're sneaking over here in the middle of the day?" she asked, laying on her Texas drawl pretty thick. "But if you don't tell him, I won't," she whispered.

"Actually, I'm here on assignment," I answered. "It's kind of important."

She looked me up and down before reaching out and running the tip of her index finger down my blue silk tie. "I know how you can get an A on that very important assignment," she cooed.

I laughed, my nerves making it a little higher than usual. She was making me very uncomfortable. "Thanks, I'll keep that in mind. I was actually here to see your nanny, Erin. She's got some connections to town that might make this plan a little easier if she was on our side."

Ivy stuck out her lip, pouting like a little girl. "I'd be happy to be on your side, or other places. I didn't grow up here, but I've made plenty of friends around town."

The woman was laying it on quite thick. "Is Erin here? It is kind of urgent I speak with her."

She rolled her eyes. "Yes, she's here. She's in the kitchen. Follow me."

I followed her through the foyer. Ivy obviously liked to dress to impress. She was wearing a pair of shorts with heels that made her legs look very long, despite her petite figure. I looked away. I didn't know what kind of marriage she and Larry had, but I did not want to get accused of messing around with my boss's wife. Maybe that's how they did things back home, but it wasn't the way I did things. Besides, the blonde hair and blue-eyed thing wasn't for me. I had eyes for only one woman.

"Erin?" Ivy called out, stepping into the massive kitchen.

"I'll be right there," I heard her call out.

A few seconds later, she emerged from a small room off the kitchen carrying a bag of flour. She froze when she saw me. I was glad as hell Ivy was looking at Erin with her back to me. I didn't want her to know how attracted I was to Erin. I stared at the woman who had been dancing through my dreams for years. She was wearing a pair of cutoff jean shorts that showed off long, tanned legs, a simple tank, and sensible tennis shoes. It was the polar opposite to Ivy's little getup and about a million times sexier.

"Hi," I said when she said nothing.

"Uh, hi," she answered.

Ivy turned to look at me, a scowl on her face as she looked back at Erin. The tension in the kitchen was palpable. There was no way Ivy didn't feel it. Erin moved to the counter and set down the bag of flour next to a large mixing bowl.

"Well, I suppose you two need to talk. Behave yourselves," she quipped before sashaying out of the kitchen.

I turned to look back at Erin, drinking in the sight of her and immediately wanting to touch her, kiss her again. She was staring at me with what I sensed was anger. She thought I was stalking her. I was—but I had a good excuse.

## 12

### ERIN

Despite my shock at seeing Jacob standing in the kitchen in front of me, I also felt relief. Ellie and the Welsh kids were at day camp, which meant I didn't have to worry about Jacob seeing her. Even without Ellie being present, there was a chance Ivy might mention my daughter. That would be awkward.

"What are you doing here?" I asked, slightly irritated by his presence.

I didn't want Ivy finding out about us. I didn't want anyone finding out. It would only lead to more questions that I didn't want to answer. Things were best left in the past.

"I have a proposition for you," he said in that smooth, deep voice as he walked toward me.

"I thought there was a no solicitor sign on the gate," I retorted.

He grinned. "Trust me, you want to hear this. It concerns you and your job here."

I raised a brow. "My job?"

"Can we sit?"

"Fine." I gestured to the table where the box of crayons was still sitting from earlier. "If it's about the other night, that has nothing to do with my job, and I would really rather not talk about it, especially here," I added in a low voice.

He looked around before leaning forward. "Western Energies is getting stonewalled. The city council won't let us move forward."

I shrugged a shoulder. "And what has that got to do with me and my job?"

"Because if Western Energies can't get the oil Larry moved here to get, he's going to close up shop and move on to another business venture. You and I both know there is nothing keeping them here. Burning Butte does not offer the type of life Ivy and Larry are accustomed to. If they pull up stakes and leave, you're out of a job and so am I," he said, completely serious.

"And why do you think I can help?" I asked.

"Because you're from here. You're the town princess. Your family is Burning Butte royalty. If you are on board with Western Energies drilling, others will fall into place. Your dad still has a lot of influence around here. If you convince him, he'll convince the others," he explained.

I wrinkled my nose. "Why don't *you* convince them it's so great? Isn't that *your* job?"

He grinned. "Turns out a lot of people still don't like me much around here."

I tried to hide my reaction. I knew why a lot of folks held a grudge against him. Everyone knew he was Ellie's father. I never came right out and said it, but everyone knew, and everyone knew he wasn't around. They assumed he knocked me up and then ran off. Few people knew the truth.

"Jacob, I think you just need to try and ask nicely. That stuff happened a long time ago. I'm sure people will be fine with you," I encouraged, knowing it was bullshit.

"I need your help, please," he insisted.

"I don't know what you want me to do. You know my dad isn't going to listen to me. He's stubborn and set in his ways," I reminded him.

He took a deep breath. "If you can't get your dad, you can at least try talking to some of the locals. Erin, this is serious. It seems like you like your job here. I know I sure as hell like my job. I need your help. I honestly don't think I can do this without you. Larry is counting on me, and I feel like I've hit a brick wall. No one is willing to give me the time of day let alone listen to anything I have to say about a company they've already decided they hate," he said.

The pleading in his voice was pulling at me. I had a feeling he knew it and was using it to his advantage. Before I could tell him I would help, Ivy's heels clopping across the marble floor interrupted us. When she appeared in the kitchen, my mouth nearly fell open, then I remembered she was my boss and hid my reaction. The woman was wearing almost nothing, strutting across the room in a tiny string bikini with all of her assets on display.

I looked at Jacob to judge his reaction and was relieved to

see he looked more uncomfortable than excited. Ivy craved attention and didn't mind getting it wherever she could, even if it was with a younger man who happened to work for her husband. I watched as she strutted to where we were sitting at the table, standing very close to Jacob, which put her boobs almost directly in line with his face. I had to fight to keep from curling my lip with disgusted rage. The string bikini covered next to nothing. As if the damn thing weren't ridiculous enough for a backyard swim, she was wearing gold bangle bracelets and a necklace with a large medallion that rested between her ample cleavage. It was meant to draw the eye. I wasn't quite so naive I didn't recognize a seduction when I saw it.

"Did you happen to bring a suit?" Ivy cooed. "We could take a little dip and cool off."

"No, ma'am," Jacob replied, looking at me.

"I could go find one of my husband's suits. You're a little taller, but I think we could make something fit, although you do seem to be a bit broader around the chest. I suppose that wouldn't matter though, would it?" she tittered.

"I'm fine, thank you," he said, looking up at her face and completely ignoring the boobs at his chin.

"It's a beautiful day for a swim," she continued.

"I have a lot of work to get done. Thanks for the offer, but maybe another time."

Ivy pouted. "Fine, but if you change your mind, you know where to find me."

She walked away from us, heading for the glass doors, sashaying her perfect hips and her pert ass that was the result of hours on the spin bike and a little bit of liposuction. Ivy had nothing to do other than work on staying beautiful. I felt jealousy race through me and tried to push it away. I didn't want what Ivy had. I liked my life, but I damn sure didn't want her to have Jacob.

"Will you do it?" Jacob asked.

"What?" I blinked, trying to tamp down the jealousy so I could focus.

"Will you consider working with me to try and win over the town? Larry wants this. He will likely ask you himself."

The idea of working with Jacob on anything was disturbing. I couldn't spend time with him. I couldn't be in close quarters with him on a regular basis. He was a distraction. Even then, sitting with him, talking to him, and having to look at him was making me feel fluttery. He had been right about the attraction never fading. It hadn't. I wanted his body. The rest of him, I wasn't as sure, but there was something about his body that I craved.

My eyes drifted to the large clock hanging on the wall. "Um, I'll think about it."

"We don't have a lot of time here, Erin."

He wasn't kidding. I had to leave to pick up the kids from camp in about fifteen minutes. "I can't work out of the house."

"That's fine," he said, holding up a hand. "Why don't you come by the office when you're not watching the kids."

I bit my lower lip and nodded. "The kids have day camp for

the next two weeks. I suppose I could make a little time. However, I need something from you."

He grinned and I rolled my eyes. "I will give you anything you want," he said in a husky voice.

"I need you to keep a low profile. Don't go around pissing anyone off. Mind your own business and quit reminding people about who you used to be," I lectured.

He scowled. "I've done no such thing. I've been a good boy. People around here just can't seem to realize I've grown up."

"Yeah, sure. You have a natural knack for pissing people off. I'll come by the office tomorrow after I drop the kids off," I told him, looking at the time again.

He nodded. "Perfect. Thank you. Larry will thank you as well. This is a big deal. I know with you on board we can at least get the people around here to listen. I'm not expecting them to jump up and down with excitement or roll out the red carpet, but a little leeway would be huge."

"I'm making no promises. You know how stubborn these people can be. You know how stubborn my *dad* can be," I said with a grimace, already imagining how that conversation was going to go.

He smirked. "And Philip. Good ol' Philip would probably prefer to burn us down, but if we go, you're out of a job."

"I can get a job elsewhere," I retorted.

He looked around the kitchen. "One like this? You'll be stuck working next to Marianne."

"Keep talking and I won't help you. Don't come in here and

act like you're all high-and-mighty because you're wearing a fancy suit. Not everyone needs to earn big bucks," I told him, my irritation evident.

"I'm sorry," he quickly apologized. "I didn't mean it as an insult. I was only saying you look good in this kitchen. This lifestyle suits you. I don't want you to have to leave a job you obviously like. I'm sorry," he said again.

"I don't either. I said I'll be there tomorrow. I need to get going," I told him, rising from the table.

He nodded, getting to his feet. We stood facing each other, looking at one another without talking. He was so damn handsome!

"I'll see you tomorrow," he said, his voice low.

"You know where the door is."

He chuckled. "I do," he said and walked away.

I let out the breath I had been holding, relieved he was gone. He was hard to look at and not want. I was treading on very dangerous ground. Being around Jacob was risky. If anyone saw us together, they would assume that he knew about Ellie. I was hoping by keeping our meetings at his office, no one would suspect I was there to see him.

Rumors were only half the problem. I needed to figure out how I was going to convince my dad that Western Energies was a good thing. I knew he loved his sleepy little town just the way it was and wouldn't be thrilled to have things shaken up by some big company. Then there was Philip. He hated Jacob and wouldn't care that the Welsh family moving hurt me. He'd want to run Jacob out of town again. He'd sent me a few text messages saying as much.

I grabbed the keys to the SUV and headed out the door to pick up the kids. I was definitely in one of those frying pan over the fire situations. Both options sucked. But I liked my job. I needed my job. If that meant sleeping with the enemy, so to speak, then I would do it. I knew I couldn't hide Ellie from him forever, but if we were on good terms, that would help soften the blow—I hoped.

I grimaced thinking about how all of that would go down. Would he rage? Would he run away? Would he be sad? I honestly thought I would never see him again. I didn't think he could be hurt by something he didn't know about. Now that he was back and claiming to want to be with me, the hurt and anger was inevitable.

# 13

## JACOB

I could smell her. Her scent was fruity and flowery and reminded me of walking through a farmer's market on a lovely spring day. I was trying my hardest not to lean over and inhale deeply. I had to play it cool. If I pushed too hard, she was going to run in the opposite direction. I leaned back in the chair I had moved into my office to create a nice conversation area without the stiffness of the desk between us. Erin was sitting across from me in an identical chair with a large coffee table between us. It was a large enough table for a body to lie on. I had to quit thinking like that, or I was going to get myself in trouble.

"If we can make a bullet list of benefits, I think that would make it easy to understand and cut out a lot of the questions," I said, watching her reaction.

"My brother isn't an idiot. He doesn't need or want an idiot's guide to Western Energies," she retorted.

I grinned. "I didn't mean to say he was an idiot. It's just an easy way to get the information out there. A lot of people are quick to stop listening when they sense long explanations coming. Concise and to the point is the way to go. We can have flyers made up and put around town."

She shrugged a shoulder. "I suppose, but how is that going to convince Philip?"

"Philip is the sheriff, and I bet he would love to be able to buy new cars for his deputies or upgrade that rickety old building the sheriff's department is in. With the revenue generated by Western Energies and the people that come to live here to work at the company, he is going to have more money to work with," I explained.

"More people, more crime," she replied.

I laughed. "Not necessarily. More development means the people here are going to be working and earning more and ultimately spending more. And, there have been studies that prove there is lower crime when there is less poverty. A rising tide lifts all boats," I said with a smile.

She nodded. "More people living here means more kids in the school. We're not a booming town, but our schools are already struggling. How would they ever be able to meet the needs of bigger class sizes?"

I nodded, happy to offer a solution. "More revenue, more taxes, easier levies and bonds passed. And money to hire more teachers. Which again leads to jobs, taxes, more money spent in the community."

"We barely have enough bus routes for the kids as it is."

"Again, more public services would be offered with an influx of cash flow. I drove down Main Street and saw a lot of empty buildings and storefronts. Imagine all of those being filled once again. Imagine people being able to buy what they need right here in Burning Butte instead of having to drive thirty miles to Minot. They'll save gas money that they can spend here," I insisted.

She had a thoughtful look on her face. I loved that we could debate without getting angry. I needed her to point out all the holes in my arguments to convince the citizens of Burning Butte that Western Energies was a good thing for them.

"None of us wants to turn into one of those other places around here," she said, referring to the oil boom that had practically transformed quaint little towns into booming cities almost overnight.

"I don't want that either. Western Energies isn't trying to pull six million barrels a month. We're looking to keep the operation relatively small but profitable. We can do that while creating jobs and promoting healthy growth that doesn't put a strain on the schools. There will need to be housing built, and all those people that have had their houses sitting on the market for years are going to find they're sitting on gold mines," I told her, thinking about some of the for sale signs I had seen coming into town.

"You bring up some really great points, and while I can certainly see the benefits to having Western Energies in town, I think we're avoiding the real problem."

"Us?" I asked, immediately ready to shut that down.

She shook her head. "No. I mean, partly, but Philip is going to be against this whole idea in principle because you're involved. He feels betrayed by you. Philip holds a grudge.

He isn't going to help you in any way, no matter if it costs me a really great job."

I knew she was right. "You don't think he would listen to you? I know he is very protective of you, which is why he hates me so damn much."

She smiled. "He does hate you. Just in case you were wondering, he *really* hates you."

I gave her a dry look. "Yeah, I figured that out the other night."

"What? What do you mean?" she asked, wide-eyed.

"I mean, he came up to me in the parking lot after you got out of my truck. He wasn't happy to see you with me."

Her hand covered her mouth. "Oh great."

"You're a grown woman, Erin. He can't dictate who you see. He couldn't dictate it back then, but I was too weak to stand up to him. I'm not now. I'm not going to let him dictate shit to me," I growled.

"It isn't that easy. You know that."

"Regardless. This isn't about us; this is about our jobs. He needs to put aside his issues and think long term. Him holding a grudge could cost the entire town. I would think he could be reasonable enough to see that," I pointed out.

She sighed, clearly not as convinced. "I don't know. Philip has a lot of anger over what happened. He's never really said much to me, but—" She stopped talking, making me think there was something else. I waited to see if she would finish her sentence, but she looked away from me, telling me she was finished.

"Erin, he'll listen to you. Feel him out. See what he wants to make this thing happen. He'll talk to you. You're about the only person I know who can get through to him—you and your dad—and I'm not putting all my eggs in *that* basket," I muttered, remembering the sheriff's threats.

"Actually, he knows you're back."

I groaned, dread filling my gut, and the thought of cold steel being slapped around my wrists floated through my mind. I had never actually been to jail, but I didn't imagine it was a pleasant experience. Arthur Maxwell was a formidable man. There was something about him that still had a way of intimidating me. I couldn't explain it, but as much as I had convinced myself I could stand up to him, I was still nervous as hell. The idea of meeting him face-to-face made me feel like that scared kid I had been when he'd threatened to ruin my life all those years ago.

"Great," I mumbled. "Should I get bail money arranged? I'm sure he's got some trumped-up charges he's been waiting to slap on me. I am not taking the fall for that tractor that ended up in the canal," I said vehemently.

She burst into laughter. "Philip already confessed to that. He doesn't seem bothered in the least by the fact you're here," she announced.

My brows shot up. "What? Seriously?"

She nodded her head. "Yep. I told him I ran into you."
"And? Did he go in search of his shotgun?"

She giggled. "Nope. I think he's getting soft in his old age. But Philip certainly isn't. He's still stubborn and mad, and I don't see him inviting you over for a beer anytime soon."

"I won't hold my breath. Any advice on how to make him love me again?" I teased.

"Oh, I have a few suggestions, but I don't think they'd work well for you," she said, her eyes dancing with mischief.

That was the Erin I remembered. She loved poking and teasing her brother until he wanted to strangle her. They had a good relationship. I envied them both. They had another person in the world that knew their life on an intimate level. I had no one to share home-life drama with. I had no one that could relate to having a drunk for a father and a mom who just didn't care enough about anything to do anything.

"He's always been a stubborn guy," I said, shaking my head.

"Remember when you teased him about that shirt? I think it was a Metallica T-shirt or something like that?" she said a bright smile on her face.

I nodded, remembering exactly the shirt she was talking about. "I told him it was ugly and old. He always wore it with those ugly-ass faded black jeans. He looked like something from the eighties. That asshole wore the same outfit every day for a month. He told me he washed it every day after school, but I didn't believe him. He only stopped wearing it when I told him I liked it," I said, shaking my head.

"Exactly my point. Philip has only gotten more stubborn and defiant with age. He always has to prove a point, and he has some serious dedication when it comes to doing just that. I gave up trying to win an argument against him a long time ago," she said, shaking her head.

I got to my feet, my hands in my pockets as I looked around the spacious office. I was slowly adding little things to make it feel like my own. I didn't want to lose it. I liked where I was at. "I have to think of something."

Erin stood up as well, not more than a couple of feet from me. "I honestly wish I could help you," she said, her voice sweet and melodic.

I turned to face her and was once again struck by her beauty. She was so pretty and so natural. Her skin was perfect, slightly tanned from being outdoors, and I detected very little makeup. Her eyes met mine, catching me staring at her. I didn't try and hide my obvious attraction for her.

I pulled my hands out of my pocket and rested one on her trim waist before reaching up to brush her hair off her shoulder. I couldn't resist kissing her. I leaned down, placing a gentle kiss on her lips. Her eyes fluttered closed as I stepped closer, pulling her body against mine as I deepened the kiss. I felt no resistance from her. Her arms went around me, one hand pressed against my back as she pulled me in closer.

The only sound in the room was the sound of our breathing and quiet moans of approval and excitement. Anytime I was alone with her, all I thought about was putting my mouth on her in some way, shape, or form. Hell, I thought about it when I wasn't alone with her. I wanted her all the time.

Her mouth opened, inviting my tongue inside to play. I could feel my arousal growing as our tongues dueled and our bodies rubbed together. It was the best kind of friction. My hands dropped lower, squeezing her ass and grinding her pelvis against my growing erection. I heard her groan and was eager to hear more. I slowly walked her backward, lowering her to the couch with me spread out over her. My hands moved under her shirt; our lips still locked together as I fondled her breast through the satin bra she wore.

Her hands squeezed my ass, pulling me against her. I was hard and ready to dive into her sweetness. I knew no one would disturb me. I had her all to myself.

## 14

### ERIN

His kisses had a way of making me forget everything. All I could think and feel was him. It was all I wanted to feel when his lips were on mine, his body covering me like the best warm blanket on an icy-cold winter night. I wanted him. I was ready for him and would worry about what all that meant later. Just then, it was me and him and the world didn't matter.

It was the ringing of his cell phone that brought me back to earth in a hurry. I pushed at his chest and scrambled to sit up on the couch. Jacob jumped up and grabbed his phone from his desk, his erection evident from my view on the couch as he stood next to his desk. I jumped up, smoothing my hair down and trying to think of an excuse to run.

"Hello?" Jacob answered.

He held up a finger, telling me to wait. I shook my head. "Philip. I'm going to try and feel him out," I whispered before rushing out the door.

I could see he wanted to say more, but I didn't want to stick around. I rushed out of his office, hoping no one noticed what felt like swollen lips and my hair in total disarray. I got into my car and quickly turned it on, blasting the AC on my face in an attempt to cool myself down from the inside out. What the hell was wrong with me? I couldn't even keep my own promises to myself. I shook my head in disgust and leaned my head against the seat.

I took a few deep breaths, trying to calm my racing heart and libido before grabbing my phone to text Philip. I was hoping he would agree to lunch. He replied almost instantly that he would be happy to meet up. I headed to the diner he had suggested, already knowing he would choose that place. I went inside and found him sitting at a table, a disappointed look on his face. Obviously, his crush wasn't working. I sat down, trying to act casual. He had inherited that cop sense from my father and was eyeing me closely, suspicion all over his face.

"What's going on?" he asked.

I shrugged a shoulder. "I wanted to have lunch. Can't a girl just want to have lunch with her big brother?" I said with an overdone smile.

"Bullshit."

"Hey! You've been working a lot, and I've been with the kids. I thought we should catch up," I said, trying to appear nonchalant.

His dark eyes bored into mine. "I know you were with him."

"What?" I choked out, my mouth suddenly dry. "With him who?" I squeaked.

"I saw you," he said. "Don't lie to me. You know I hate that."

"And?" I questioned somewhat defiantly. "So what if I was?"

"He's nothing but trouble; always has been and always will be. You can do better than him."

I rolled my eyes. "Really? Do you have a list of eligible bachelors here in Burning Butte?" I asked sarcastically.

"You know what I mean. There are better men than him. Go out with anyone except him," he grumbled.

"You don't know anything about him anymore Phillip. What if he isn't the same guy that left town all those years ago?" I asked.

"A leopard doesn't change its spots." I tapped my fingers on the table impatiently. "Philip, I'm not a kid. I don't need you babysitting me. I can make my own decisions about who I hang out with. You are supposed to be the sheriff of the entire town, not just me. Don't you have citizens you should be protecting and serving?" I quipped.

"I watch out for you on my own time."

"In your government-issued car," I snapped.

He didn't say anything. He looked at me as if I were a little kid who was asking for ice cream for breakfast. Before I could lay into him and let him know just how stupid that was, the waitress appeared. We each quickly ordered burgers and fries before I turned my attention back to him.

"Don't," he said before I could get a word out.

"Don't what?"

"Don't tell me you're seeing him again," he growled.

"Why do you care?" I snapped.

He took a drink from his glass of cola. "I've been watching him."

My eyebrows shot up. "You've what? Like stalking him? Surveilling him?"

"I heard he was back in town and wanted to see what he was up to. I don't trust him. He might come back and look all slick in his fancy suits and driving his fancy truck, but I know his type."

I rolled my eyes. "Oh, for Christ sake, Phillip. Well?"

He scowled. "Well what?"

"What has he been up to?" I asked, trying to get my brother to admit that there was nothing sneaky happening with Jacob. He sighed. "Nothing. He's the VP at the new Western Energies outside of town. He was staying at the inn, but I heard he just found a house to rent and is looking to buy. He goes to work and home. Oh, and sometimes he goes drinking with my little sister," he said, giving me a dirty look.

"We didn't go drinking. I was out. He showed up. Again, that isn't your business," I said.

"It is."

"Honestly, Philip, he was your best friend at one time. Are you ever going to get over it? It was eight years ago. Ever thought of moving on?" I snapped.

"Nope," he replied, sipping on his drink.

"Ridiculous," I muttered under my breath.

He glowered. "The guy has never even apologized for what he did to me."

I closed my eyes, praying for patience. I had to be nice. I needed him to be fair so I could keep my job. Philip had been making the situation all about him since it all came out. "Poor you," I grumbled.

Neither of us spoke for several minutes. Thankfully, our meals were delivered a few minutes later, giving us a good excuse not to talk. I wasn't hungry, but I still had to broach the subject of why I wanted to see him in the first place.

"He could have said he was sorry," he started again.

"Sorry for what exactly?" I asked, genuinely curious to know why he felt he deserved an apology.

"For betraying me. You know that."

I couldn't do it. I couldn't keep biting my tongue. I was sick and tired of listening to him cry, whine, and pout over what Jacob had done to *him*. I dropped the half-eaten fry back on my plate and very purposefully wiped my hands on my napkin, trying my hardest to calm the anger.

"Seriously, he was supposed to be my best friend. It's guy code—you don't sleep with a guy's little sister," he pouted.

"Stop it," I hissed.

"Excuse me? Stop what?"

"Stop being such a little brat! You've been walking around with your knuckles dragging on the ground and whining about your best friend betraying you for eight years. Get over it! You're not the one who is raising a little girl on your own because your Neanderthal brother chased off the father of her child! You're not the one who lost something important! I'm so absolutely sick of hearing you complain. Man up. Quit bitching, and find a new fucking friend," I snapped, tossing the napkin on my plate and stomping out of the restaurant.

His face had been filled with shock and surprise. I hadn't said anything to him in the past. I had let him cry and bitch, keeping everything I felt locked down tight. God forbid I have any feelings about what he and my father had done to my life by butting in. I got in the car, slamming the door hard and speeding out of the parking lot. He could give me a damn ticket if he wanted to. I didn't care. I did not fucking care anymore.

I started the drive out to the Welsh mansion, passing the building where the sheriff's office was housed. It was a dose of reality seeing the old wooden building with a metal roof. It was old and had been the sheriff's office for more than fifty years. The roof was new, but the building was the same, just like so many of the other buildings lining the street. Things didn't change often in Burning Butte. There was no way I was going to get Philip to agree to welcoming Western Energies and Jacob with open arms.

He was a lost cause, and I just didn't have the patience or energy to try and persuade him. Being with Jacob and getting to know him all over again was serving to remind me of all that I had been missing. Not just me—Ellie. I was done trying to be nice to Philip. He would never agree to be a part of the welcoming committee so he could fuck off.

It was time to shift gears and rethink our plan of attack. I parked my car, sitting inside for a few minutes. My day had not gone like I thought it would have. I had thought about telling my brother just how I felt about the whole situation about a thousand times, but I never said a word because I didn't think I had a right to. He had made me feel guilty about the situation, like it was my fault his best friend left. He'd blamed me for flirting with Jacob and ultimately destroying his friendship.

It wasn't until recently I realized that it had been *his* choice to ruin that friendship. He was the one that had the big hang-up. He had loved Jacob like a brother. Why was it so bad that I had fallen for him?

I couldn't answer those questions, and I didn't think he could either. That was a problem for another day. For now, I had to think of a way to keep not only my job, but Jacob's. I knew Philip was set on getting Jacob out of town for good this time. He wouldn't care if it disrupted my life. It hadn't stopped him the first time, and it wouldn't stop him this time. I was collateral damage. He would reason Ellie and I could move back home with dad and I could get a job at a restaurant or something.

I stomped up the stairs to my apartment and walked inside, looking around at the space and realizing if I didn't think of something and fast, I wouldn't get to have my own place again. I would never find a job in Burning Butte making enough money to rent a house for me and Ellie. Lord knew I would never be able to actually buy my own home.

## 15

## JACOB

I loosened my tie as I walked outside the two-story building. It felt more like a noose than an accessory, choking me. The blazing heat of the day had me stripping off my suit jacket, hooking it on my finger, and slinging it over my shoulder as I walked down the sidewalk to my truck. My meeting had gone to shit. It had been a last-ditch effort to get someone on our side—someone to give us the go-ahead to move forward with the plans.

I could practically see my future going up in smoke. Everything I had worked so hard for was falling apart. I could get another job in another city, but it wasn't what I wanted. It defeated the purpose of me coming back to Burning Butte. I couldn't very well convince Erin I could support her and give her a good life if I was unemployed. Sure, I would have a fancy diploma to hang on the wall, but that wouldn't mean shit in Burning Butte. The city manager wasn't confident we would ever get our company off the ground. He was on board with it, but we needed a lot more than just his support. The guy was a little soft around the edges in my opinion. With him at the helm, Burning Butte would never grow, never prosper. I wasn't a politician, but someone with some vision needed to step up and run the show instead of relying on the way things had always been done. The city manager was scared to make waves. Waves made life interesting in my opinion. He had told me too many townspeople had already come forward to make their opinions very clear on the matter. They resented some rich out-of-towners coming in trying to shake things up. If it were a local making the changes, they'd be all for it, but in their eyes, Larry Welsh was a rich man trying to get richer off the backs of hardworking people. I apparently didn't count as a local, which didn't exactly hurt my feelings.

I was almost to my truck when something caught my eye. I walked through the door and headed directly for the counter where Erin was staring down at the glass.

I stepped behind her and covered her eyes with my hands. "Guess who?" I said close to her ear.

She nearly jumped three feet in the air before spinning around and staring at me wild-eyed. "Jacob!" she exclaimed. "You're here!"

"Hi. Yes, I'm here," I said, wondering why she was acting like I had approached her wielding a chainsaw.

She looked down at three kids standing beside her. I realized they must be the Welsh kids. I had thought Larry said he had two kids, but I had obviously misheard him. "Who's that?" a little girl with long brown hair and striking hazel eyes asked Erin.

Her brother and sister were looking at me with curious

expressions on his face. "My name is Jacob. I'm an old friend of Erin's," I said with a smile.

The girl at the counter was looking at me expectantly. I ordered a double scoop of Rocky Road. Erin was standing shell-shocked in front of the register. I pulled out a twenty and paid for all of the ice cream.

"Thank you," she murmured.

"Of course. Do you have a minute?" I asked.

She looked down at the kids. "I should probably get them home."

"You just gave them ice cream cones," I reminded her. "Do you really want those in the car?"

She smiled, still looking unsure. "You're right. Sure." She turned to the kids, ushering them to one of the red tables and gesturing for me to sit at the one directly behind the kids.

"Thanks."

"What's up?" she asked, her tongue popping out as she licked the strawberry ice cream. It was doing all sorts of things to my body that we not appropriate in a family setting. "I just left a meeting with the city manager."

She grimaced. "Uh-oh. I take it didn't go well?"

I shook my head. "No. Not at all. He basically laughed me out of his office. He's okay with our plans and is actually thrilled with the idea of a little growth and what it could mean to the town. It's everyone else that's putting up a big fight."

The little girl with the long brown hair got out of her seat and came to stand next to Erin. "You're not eating your ice cream," she said pointedly.

I looked at the cone in my hand and smiled. "I guess I'm not. I was too busy talking."

"Do you want a different flavor?" she asked.

I shook my head. "I love Rocky Road."

She held up her ice cream. "My favorite is mint chocolate chip."

"I love ice cream too," I agreed.

"I like ice cream almost as much as I like my best friends," she said, nodding her head.

My eyebrows shot up. "Really? That's pretty serious. I think I might like ice cream more than I like my friends," I said with a laugh. "I wonder if there is a way to make the people around here like Larry Welsh as much as they like ice cream," I joked, looking at Erin.

Erin took a bite of her ice cream and then froze, slapping her hand on the table. "Brain freeze?" I asked with a grimace.

She shook her head. "No! That's it. That's what we can do!"

"What?" I asked, completely confused, wondering what I had missed.

She bobbed her head up and down in that way she did when she was excited. "We'll have an ice cream social. It will be a meet and greet and let people get to know Larry and his family. They'll see that he is a good, family man with their best interests at heart. Granted, he'll make a lot of money, but I bet he will be willing to give back to the community."

I nodded my head, letting the idea resonate. "You're right. That's a great idea. We'll buy all the ice cream from here, keep the money local. It will give everyone an idea about what money can do for their hometown."

"Exactly. It'll be a relaxed environment. No one is going to have an agenda pushed down their throat. They can talk, like really talk and just get to know him and the company and even you," she said with a smile.

"Maybe I shouldn't go," I said.

She slowly shook her head. "No. You need to be there. You are a part of the company, and you're going to be spending more time with them than Larry. You have to start somewhere. I think you'll find people will be far more receptive to you when you strip off the suit and just be you. You don't have to prove anything to anyone." Her tone was gentle.

It was a little difficult to have a real conversation with a kid standing there hanging on every word, but fortunately, we knew each other well enough I could kind of read between the lines. I knew what she was saying. I had come on too strong. I was trying to be the proverbial rags-to-riches story, flaunting all my success with my tailored suits and five-hundred-dollar shoes. It was too much. I immediately felt like an asshole.

"You're right. Jeans, cold beer, and lots of ice cream," I said, nodding.

The little girl wrinkled her nose. "Beer? Nobody wants beer."

"Men do," I told her.

Erin nodded. "I think beer is a great idea. It will make the townspeople feel like you're one of them. Larry too."

"Do you really think it will work?" I asked hopefully.

"Everybody likes ice cream," the little girl said. "And everyone likes new friends."

Erin smiled at the girl, patting her on the shoulder. "Will you please go sit with Mackenzie and Mitchell?"

The girl nodded and bounced back to the table. "She's smart. She must get that from her dad," I commented.

Erin looked like she was going to vomit. "She did," she muttered.

"I think it's a good idea. Larry will love it," I told her. "Thank you for helping me out. I've been kind of struggling here."

"Thank you for warning me about what was coming," she said.

I ate my ice cream, thinking about the upcoming social. "I did come on kind of high-and-mighty, huh?"

She shrugged. "You had a hard time when you were here last. I get it. You wanted to prove you had made it, exceeded all of them in wealth, and weren't the guy you were when you left. We all dream of doing that. We all want to come home after being gone a long time and have something to show for it. You're not the first person to leave Burning

Butte and come back with an education and a step up in life. With that said, you are one of the first to come back with a chip on your shoulder."

"I don't—" I stopped. I did. She knew me too well.

"I don't blame you. I think I would have a hell of a chip on my shoulder too after what happened to you," she grumbled.

"I'll do better," I said, nodding.

"I know you will. I have to get these guys back home."

"Will you come by tomorrow?" I asked her.

She nodded. "I will. I'll drop them off at camp and head over."

"Thank you, Erin," I said, wishing like hell I could touch her or give her a kiss goodbye.

She rose and wiped the hands of each kid before leading them out the door. I liked watching her with the kids. She was good with them. I could see how much they liked her as well. Larry couldn't have gotten any luckier with another nanny. Watching her with the kids made me want to try even harder to make the Western Energies thing work. Those kids needed her as much as she needed the job. I could swallow my pride, strip away the cool veneer I had been wearing since I'd first graduated from business school.

I tossed the remaining bit of my ice cream cone in the trash and headed for my truck. I felt a million times better now that we had a plan. I was sure it would work. Larry was a very personable man, and if they would give him a chance, I was sure they would see he was a good man. I had to get his foot in the door.

I wasn't looking forward to telling Larry about the meeting with the city manager, but I wouldn't lie to him. We were still in for an uphill battle, but at least now we had a chance.

## 16

### ERIN

The term playing with fire was totally apt for my situation. After the run-in with Jacob at the ice cream shop, I should have learned a lesson. It should have been a wake-up call that parading his daughter right under his nose was only going to end badly. Every damn time I spoke with him and didn't tell him about her, I was making the situation a little worse. Like the ice cream shop. Ellie was right in front of him, talking to him, and he had no idea he was talking to his daughter. I felt horrible that he didn't know, and the longer I kept it from him, the worse it was going to be when he found out. I just couldn't bring myself to say it. If only Hallmark made a card or there was a book that gave pointers about how to tell a dude 'surprise, you're the proud daddy of a seven-year-old.'

Thankfully, Jacob didn't ask questions about Ellie. It was as if it never occurred to him I could have gotten pregnant. If she would have called me mom, I wondered if he would have put it together. The job situation was definitely occupying his thoughts for the time being, but once that was settled, he might come up for air and really look around and notice the little girl who bore a striking resemblance to him. Instead, he seemed to take it all in stride that I was hanging out with three kids. Maybe he didn't know how many kids Larry had, or maybe he thought she was a tagalong. When she had actually talked with him, I had thought for sure the jig was up. I thought he'd recognize himself in her. He didn't or he didn't mention it.

"Do you think that will work?" he asked.

I blinked, looking up from the yellow pad I had in my lap. I had been staring at the word chocolate for too long. My eyes were blurred from staring and not blinking as I mulled over the Ellie situation. We'd been in his office working up a plan for the ice cream social for a couple of hours and were making good progress, but it didn't stop my mind from drifting. I kept waiting for him to tell me he knew and was waiting for me to tell him. I kept waiting for the other shoe to drop, for him to rage at me before storming out, never to be seen again.

"Yes," I blurted out, not entirely sure what I was saying yes to.

"Larry was thrilled with the idea. I gave you all the credit," he said with a smile. "He's anxious to meet people and show them he isn't really the big bad wolf they're making him out to be."

"Thank you for telling him it was my idea, but you're doing a lot of the work on this," I told him with a smile.

"Do you think we'll be able to get your dad or Philip to go?" he questioned, his mouth set in a tight line.

I shrugged. "I think my dad will go, but I wouldn't count on Philip, at least not to be a help to the situation. If he goes, I imagine it would only make things worse. He might rile people up and completely disrupt the plan of having a casual event."

He groaned, leaning back in his chair. "Great. Why don't we cordially disinvite him?" he said with a chuckle.

I rolled my eyes. "Oh, yeah, because that will make it so much better when he shows up uninvited and pissed."

"Maybe I should just let him hit me and get it over with," he grumbled.

"That's not a terrible idea," I offered, earning a scowl from him.

"Whose side are you on?" he asked, looking me in the eyes. I didn't answer. "Never mind," he said with a sigh.

The easy nature vanished with the subject of Philip hanging between us. "We'll have to work on this tomorrow. I've got to get the kids picked up," I said, checking the time and looking for any excuse to leave.

"We have a lot to get done. I need to get this social planned as soon as possible. Every day we're not moving forward, we're burning money," he said. "Is there any way you can have someone pick them up?"

"No. I'm the nanny, remember?" I said, a little irritated he would even suggest it.

"Sorry. Why don't I come by the house in an hour or so?" he offered.

I shook my head. I couldn't have him around Ellie or the

Welsh family in general. The risk of them mentioning she was my daughter was too great. "I can come back tomorrow after I drop them off," I told him.

"Can we have dinner tonight—strictly business," he quickly added. "I don't want to put you out, but this is so important."

I grimaced. "I can't. I don't get to punch out at five o'clock. There's dinner and baths and the general craziness. I think the Welshes might have plans later," I mumbled, not technically lying but not knowing for sure. I was terrified to spend time with him. What if my secret slipped? What if he was testing me and I was failing? What if he knew about Ellie and she was the real reason he came back?

"Erin, I don't have to tell you how important this is for both of us. We've got a good start. We could have this thing in a couple of weeks if we can finalize the details. Larry is anxious to get the permit process started. That is going to take weeks, possibly months. Every single day is truly costing thousands," he said, stressing the word. "A couple hours, please?" he pleaded.

"I get it, but I have a job. I can't up and leave the kids. I'm working to keep the job I have. I'm not trying to lose it by shirking my duties. They need me."

He rubbed his hands over his face. "I get it, I do. What time do they go to bed?"

I laughed. "You're persistent."

"I am. You know I am. This is important to me, and I never give up on anything I really want."

I thought about it, staring at the pleading in his eyes, and was helpless to deny him. He had a warmth, a depth to him that I had never found in anyone else. It was like there was an invisible thread connecting the two of us. I felt like I understood him better than anyone else in the world.

"Okay," I heard myself say.

"Okay?"

I let out a sigh. "Yes. It won't be until after eight. I need to get the kids settled and make sure it's okay with Larry and Ivy."

"Perfect," he said, jumping up and going to his desk. I watched as he wrote something down on a piece of paper before handing it to me. "My address. I'll see you then."

I stuck the paper in my pocket, telling myself I was only taking it because it was important to keeping my job. It wasn't because I wanted to see him. I got into the Welsh SUV and headed for the church where the kids were finishing up their final days of camp.

I got back to the mansion and went about our usual routine, making dinner and playing a few games with the kids. I pulled Ellie to the side before dinner.

"You're going to have a sleepover at Grandpa's house tonight," I told her.

She grinned. "Yeah! We can work on our birdhouse!"

"Yes, you can, but you can't stay up late," I warned her.

I knew my words were falling on deaf ears. All bets were off when it came to Grandpa's house. With the other kids settled in, I packed Ellie a little overnight bag and took her to my dad's house.

"To what do I owe this lovely gift?" he asked.

"I have a new project I'm working on. It's important and I need to put in the time to make sure it's perfect," I told him.

He smiled. "A project, huh?" he asked.

"Yes, Dad. I'm not saying any more. I'll be by in the morning. I don't want to wake her after she's gone to bed," I said, trying to sound completely rational.

"It's no problem. You have a good night," he said with that knowing smile.

I walked to my car, a little weirded out that my dad knew what I was up to, even if I didn't tell him. It was that cop sixth sense. I double-checked the address Jacob had given me and pointed the car in the right direction. I parked in the driveway of the newer house in a quiet part of town. I remembered when we had talked about living in the good part of town in one of the fancy houses. He'd achieved his dream. I was proud of him.

I knocked on the door. When he opened it, he was wearing a pair of worn jeans and a T-shirt that looked like it had been washed a hundred times. The man standing in front of me was the man I remembered from eight years ago. It was the rough-and-tough guy I had fallen for so long ago. This was the man I wanted everyone else to see. Or maybe not. I kind of liked the idea of keeping him all to myself.

"Come in," he said, opening the door wide.

"Thanks," I murmured, turning sideways to avoid touching him as I walked into his house.

I looked around the living room. It was a nice house, big and roomy with an open floor plan. I could see the kitchen, dining room, and living room from where I stood just inside the doorway. Whoever had made the idea trendy was a genius. It was so much easier to be able to watch the kids while making dinner or cleaning up the kitchen without walls blocking the view.

"Can I get you anything? Water, beer, wine?" he asked.

"Um, I wouldn't mind some wine," I said, figuring one glass early in the night would be okay.

"Great. Come in. We can sit at the table or in the living room, whatever you prefer," he offered.

"The table works," I said, wanting to keep it professional.

The couch was risky. We couldn't be on the couch. I was already having a hard enough time trying to fight off my need to touch him. I inwardly chided myself for showing up at all. I knew there was an electric attraction between us, and being in his house, alone, after dark, was dangerous. Maybe I was a glutton for punishment, or maybe I wanted to test my resolve. I didn't know why I agreed to show up, but it was stupid and dangerous and fantastic.

"Here you go," he said, handing me a glass of white wine.

We moved to the table where he had a couple of pens and yellows pad already sitting. I took a seat, hoping he'd sit far away from me. He didn't. He sat down on my left, our elbows nearly touching. I could feel his body heat, smell his cologne, and knew I was in for a long evening. It would be a test of my resolve. I resolved not to get caught up in Jacob's orbit—not again. I couldn't survive the fallout when he left me again.

# 17

## JACOB

My body was misbehaving. I couldn't stop the hormones from dumping into my bloodstream like a dam opening the floodgates. It was pure arousal burning through my veins. Every little thing she did was turning me on. Sitting next to her, smelling her, listening to her breath—all of it. All of it was sexy as hell and making me crazy.

"Focus," I breathed the word.

"What?" Erin asked, turning to look at me.

I shook my head, a little embarrassed I had actually said it out loud. "Nothing. Sorry," I murmured.

She let out a breath and leaned back, holding up the paper she'd been writing on. "Okay, I think this will work for a poster to get people to the social. Like you said before, we'll keep it simple with bullet points instead of long sentences."

"And the beer garden idea? Do you think that's okay, or are we blurring the line between family-friendly and a party?" I asked, still not sure if it was a good idea.

"Most of the people around her like cold beer, and the kids are used to seeing their parents have a beer or two at a back-yard barbecue. I think you have to appeal to the whole crowd, and the men are going to be more inclined to come for free beer than they would be for free ice cream," she reasoned.

I nodded. "Okay. I've started a list of things I'll need to do to make that happen. Hopefully, they will let us serve alcohol," I grumbled, knowing it was probably another fight we had in front of us.

Erin laughed, that soft, airy sound that sent shivers up and down my spine. "It's beer. That's the one thing none of those guys is going to fight. Free beer isn't something anyone is going to pass up. You should be able to get a temporary license without too much trouble."

"If you say so," I mumbled, trying to keep my head on the task at hand, but being in such close proximity to her for so long was making it next to impossible.

Her smile faded and she looked at me with those eyes that said she wanted me. It'd been the same look she'd been giving me all night, but the moment I thought about acting on it, she pulled away. I didn't dare push it and risk having her run out the door. I had been tamping down the lust, and it was getting to the point it wouldn't be ignored much longer.

"I'll call that place that has those bounce house things. That will be a great way to keep the kids distracted while the adults talk business," she said, pulling her gaze away from mine and back to the paper.

I swallowed the lust and focused on the task at hand.

"Great. Now we need to find a venue. I think we need an indoor/outdoor situation. It's hot and I don't want people to be uncomfortable."

She grimaced, shaking her head. "We don't have anything like that. What about getting a couple of those big tents they use for weddings?" she suggested.

"I don't know, that might be worse. We could get big fans, I suppose, to try and keep things cool," I said, already jotting it down.

"You're really pulling out all the stops here," she said, turning to look at me once again.

"I am. Like I've said, this is important. There's a lot riding on this one little ice cream social. You only get one chance to make a good first impression. In the case of Western Energies, we're getting a second chance. Larry should have talked with the town leaders before he started buying up land and drilling rights. He knows better now. It's time to do a little backtracking and start over. This has to work. I don't want to work for anyone else," I told her.

"Have you worked anywhere else?" she asked.

"A few places, but the business world in the city is cutthroat. Everyone is so damn competitive, and very few men have the morals Larry does. I was in New York for a while and was making great money, but I felt like I had sold my soul to the devil. I couldn't keep doing it. I took a huge chance by going to a conference where I ended up meeting Larry. I had gone in the hopes of feeling out some other companies to see if I could find a better job, and it worked."

She smiled and nodded her head. "He is a good guy. When

I first read the advertisement for a nanny job, I thought the person must have put the ad in the wrong paper. Burning Butte does not have families that have nannies. I figured I would apply anyway, more out of curiosity. At the time, they hadn't bought the mansion yet. They were looking into it, but they wanted to make sure the kids would be taken care of. Ivy goes back to Dallas a lot, and she is the head of probably at least a dozen charities. I met her first and a few days later, Larry flew up here just to meet me. I liked him right away. He seemed genuine and very easy to get along with. The rest is history."

"I got that same first impression, and I think the people around here will as well, if they give him a chance. The guy is filthy rich, but he hasn't let it go to his head. Ivy on the other hand..." I said, leaving the words hanging.

Erin threw her head back and laughed. Her neck stretched and revealed a stretch of smooth skin begging to be kissed. I reined it in. I could be good. I could be near her and not want her naked under me.

"Ivy is a charmer when she wants to be. I'll talk to her and let her know she'll need to dial it back a little. She's the head of several charities for a reason. She knows how to woo people. She was a born schmoozer and can be very sweet, funny, and charming when she wants to be. She's also a hell of a flirt," she said with a grimace.

I nodded. "Yes, I know."

"Do you know who she reminds me of sometimes?" Erin said out of the blue.

I shrugged a shoulder. "I have no idea."

She grinned, her eyes lighting up. "Remember that time we snuck out—"

I cut her off, reaching out and pushing her hair away from her shoulder. "You have to be specific. We snuck out a lot."

She playfully slapped my hand away. "I wasn't finished. We snuck out to go to some concert in Bismarck. You had seen some weird posters around town, and that little adventurous side of you had to know what it was all about. You got me that fake ID so I could go with you."

I grinned. "I do remember."

"It was a female rock band. The lead singer looked a lot like Ivy. Remember she wore that skirt that was nothing more than an ACE bandage, and her tiny string bikini top looked close to bursting? The woman couldn't sing at all, but when she finished her first set and she came off stage to get a drink, she was the nicest, most normal person in the world," she said, shaking her head in disbelief.

I laughed. "Normal, maybe, but her choice of outfit was ridiculous. And she could not sing worth shit."

Erin laughed again. "Yeah, I don't think we watched her second set."

In a moment, the laughter died on both of our lips as we both traveled back in time. "No, we didn't. We ended up in the men's room of that dirty bar. I had you pressed against the wall, making out like only young people can when a security guard came in."

She nodded; her eyes locked with mine. "They checked our IDs, realized mine was a really bad fake, and tossed us out."

"That five minutes in the bathroom of that sleazy bar was one of the best moments of my life. I can still taste the cherry Chapstick"

Her eyes dropped to my mouth and then back to look at me. "That was a wild night."

Her tongue darted out to lick her lips. I knew what she was thinking. I was thinking the same thing. The undeniable attraction between us was still there, just as powerful as it had been in the bar that night. We'd been crazy and reckless, and the thought of being together overpowered all rational thought. I reached for her, my hand going to the back of her head and pulling her forward as I went in for the kiss. She didn't taste like cherry Chapstick, but the wine on her lips was just as sweet. Everything came flooding back in that moment. All the hopes and dreams and excitement that came with young love was still fresh in my mind. It was all there. I felt the same way about her now as I did back then, but on a much more intense level.

Our kiss turned frantic, much like it had been in the front seat of my truck that night. Her hands were running up and down my back, her nails digging deep through my T-shirt as her need turned feral. I was all too eager to answer the call. I wrapped an arm around her waist and pulled her to her feet, kicking the chair I had been sitting in back and out of my way.

"I have to fucking have you," I growled, reaching for her blouse and yanking it up.

"Me too," she gasped, her hands fumbling with my shirt.

I tossed her shirt to the floor and quickly yanked mine off before pulling her against me so hard it pushed the air from her lungs. I was happy to give her a little mouth to mouth. I crushed my mouth to hers, sucking her tongue inside as my hand worked her bra, unhooking it and freeing her breasts.

"Fuck me," I groaned, reaching between us to cup her breasts, feeling the pebbled nipples rock hard. She was as aroused as I was.

Her nails scraped down my bare back. I arched against her as she scored my flesh. I reached for the button on her shorts, quickly getting it undone and pushing them down her legs with a furious jerking motion. Her hands moved to the button fly of my jeans, fumbling to get them undone. I pushed her hands away, taking care of the task myself. I kicked off my shoes and shucked my jeans before stripping out of my boxers.

Her soft little hand wrapped around me, squeezing my erection and damn near making me explode in her hand. I reached between her legs, parting her folds and pushing a finger in, finding her wet and hot and oh so ready for me.

"You're so wet," I whispered.

"I want you," she groaned.

We'd been waiting too long already, I decided. I didn't want to wait another second. My hand reached out, pushing the wineglasses, notepads, and pens away. They scattered to the floor as I cleared the table in a hurry. I reached for her waist, lifted her, and dropped her on the rented kitchen table before moving my hand right back to the warmth waiting for me between her legs. My fingers parted her folds once again. It was mere seconds before she was orgasming, arching and crying out for more.

I needed to feel her around me. I nudged her legs wider and stepped between them, pulling her to the edge of the table and pushing myself inside her sweet heat. Her arms went around my neck, holding me close as our bodies joined together in beautiful rapture. I never wanted to move or leave where I was right then. I could die a happy man with her holding me tight.

## 18

### ERIN

I was a fool. I knew I should have told him no. I should have walked out the door. I shouldn't have ever shown up in the first place. He shifted his stance, and all thoughts of leaving vanished. I groaned, little aftershocks spiraling through my body as he moved inside me.

"God damn, you feel so good," he whispered close to my ear.

I turned to kiss him, forcing him to open his mouth while I explored the depths with my tongue. My breasts were pressed against his chest, tiny little crinkly hairs scraping over my sensitive nipples. I rubbed against him, enjoying the sensation of being fully embraced by him.

"More," I told him in a husky voice.

"I feel like I've died and gone to heaven," he rasped.

"Not yet, you haven't."

He growled low in his chest before reaching around me and

hoisting me off the table, his heavy shaft still buried inside me as he began to move. Every step he took bounced me on him, heightening my arousal and taking me close to another orgasm. It was so much better with him than I remembered. It felt good and right and like everything sex with a man was supposed to be.

He carried me out of the kitchen and down a short hall. He kicked open a door, the room dark as he made his way across the carpeted floor to the bed. He gently placed me on the bed, standing up and staring down at me in the darkness. I looked back at him, admiring the height and the strength of his body.

"I've dreamed about having you in a bed for a long time," he breathed.

I smiled. "There's always a first time for everything."

He grinned. "There are so many firsts I want to have with you."

"What are you waiting for?" I asked in a sultry voice, feeling free and uninhibited in the moment.

His body covered mine, one hand going around me, lifting me up and scooting me higher on the bed before he plunged inside me again. I groaned with the exquisite pleasure of being filled by him. Our bodies melded together as if they had been made to fit together exactly as we were. He gave me his all, teasing and tantalizing and taking me to the brink of orgasm before pulling back, refusing to give me what I needed to fall over the edge.

"I've wanted you for so long," he whispered, breathing

heavy as he propped himself up on his elbows and looked down at me.

I didn't know how to answer him. I stuck with the truth. "I want you too. It's always been you. It's your body I crave, your touch, your gentle kisses, and the way you know how to tease me."

He leaned down and kissed me before beginning a slow, burning grind of his body into mine. I could feel him putting all of his passion and energy into the movement. It was an assault of the best kind. My senses were all heightened. Everything felt intensified, magnified a million times. Every nerve was firing off, sending delicious sensations of pure pleasure through my body. I cried out, whimpering and begging for more while telling him to stop at the same time. It was too good. I didn't know anything could ever feel so good. My second orgasm was violent and beautiful and full of rapture. In that moment, I knew I would never experience that kind of pure pleasure with anyone. Ever. Only him.

When he finally surrendered to his own need and we were both gasping and crying out, I knew I was in trouble. It felt so good and so right with him. No man could ever make me feel the way he did. Not physically and not emotionally. He dropped onto his back, pulling me against him as we both basked in the aftermath of what I was going to declare the best sex I ever had. His hand slowly stroked up and down my arm. It was something he used to do when we sat outside in the middle of the night, both of us cold, but neither of us wanting to leave and go back to our own warm beds. Those nights out under the stars were the only time we could be together. It was worth enduring a little cold to be with him. Back then, he'd rubbed my arms to help keep me warm. It had become a part of our routine. Just then, lying in his bed, it was anything but chilly, but it was soothing and lulling me into a place of complete relaxation. Neither of us said a word as we held each other.

I wondered what he was thinking about. Was he thinking about me? His work? Maybe he was planning our future together like he used to do. I was afraid of the future. Afraid of what it would look like when he realized he'd been pushed out of Burning Butte and the life of his child. I mulled over the many regrets I had been racking up, especially in the last two weeks since he'd been back in town. Every day I didn't tell him was another day of regret. Every time I looked into his eyes and said nothing, I felt awful. How could I ever expect to have anything with him if I couldn't talk to him about the one thing in my life that was more important than anything else?

All the thinking about my mistakes was exhausting. His hand was still caressing my arm, calming my mind. Before I knew it, I had fallen into a point of utter relaxation and couldn't move if I tried. I let my eyes fall closed, promising myself it would only be for a few minutes, then I would get up and go home. He made me feel safe and warm and cared about, something I hadn't felt before. In Jacob's arms, the rest of the problems in the world didn't matter. He was the best warm blanket a girl could have. I snuggled against him, inhaling the smell of him.

There was no way I could deny what had happened without me even realizing it was happening. I'd gone and fallen head over heels in love with him all over again. I wasn't sure I had ever stopped loving him, even if I had been furious with him for a long time. It was not what I wanted to happen. I didn't want to love him. It was dangerous. I knew better and yet, with him, I lost all good sense. I let my heart lead the way and ignored all that my brain was telling me.

I jerked awake sometime later. The feeling of a man's arms around me had been foreign and sent alarm racing down my spine before I remembered where I was. I had no idea how long I had slept for but knew I didn't want to be there in the morning. I very carefully disentangled myself from his arms and quietly tiptoed out of his room. I picked up my scattered clothes and quickly dressed, before picking up the glasses and notepads and putting them back on the table. That was a memory I would not soon forget. It was the kind of thing I had seen in the movies but never expected to actually live through. I turned off the lights and locked the door behind me.

Once in the car, I rolled down the window to take advantage of the cool evening air. I loved him. It was more of an acknowledgement of something I had known for a long time but tried to pretend wasn't there. I had tried to accept my father's explanation it was nothing more than a teenage crush and I would get over it. I had told myself over and over I would find someone else that made my heart sing and my body hum. I hadn't. After what happened last night, I knew without a doubt I never would. There was no other man that could ever make me feel like he did.

Which brought me right back around to the one thing standing in our way of being happy together. It wasn't Philip. It was my secret. Technically, not a secret, but I had certainly not been open and honest. I had to tell him about

Ellie. Only then would I allow myself to think about a relationship with him. I had spent some time with him, and I did feel like he had changed, matured a lot, and was serious about settling down. I had no real reason not to tell him. He wasn't violent or cruel and had done nothing to make me think he wasn't a good person.

I couldn't expect him to be ready for a kid. Few people had the luxury of actually being ready. I wasn't ready, but it happened, and it was the best thing in the world. I was hoping that's how he would feel as well. If he didn't, if he decided he wasn't interested in a ready-made family, I would give Philip the green light to run his ass out of town again. This time, I would make damn sure he knew not to come back. I would not let him hurt my little girl by rejecting her. Hell, I wouldn't need Philip to run him out of town; I would do it myself.

I drove up the long drive to the mansion and parked my car in the garage. It felt weird to be in the apartment alone, but it was probably good that I was. I needed to figure out what to do. Not what to do, but how to do it. I already knew he had to know about Ellie.

I undressed and pulled on the old pajama shorts and shirt and crawled between the covers. I stared up at the ceiling and thought about what Jacob had said about fate bringing us together. Larry had appeared in both our lives at the exact right time. Maybe fate wasn't finished yet. The idea of sitting back and letting someone else take the reins was very appealing. I liked the idea of fate having some grand plan to reveal Ellie to Jacob. It would be the exact right thing at the exact right time, just like Jacob meeting Larry at that conference and me answering the ad. Those little chance encounters in our lives had brought us back together.

I smiled, content with the idea of letting things unfold as they should. I couldn't and wouldn't force the issue. Jacob's response to the knowledge of his daughter would be right, no matter if that meant he left Burning Butte for good or if he stayed. I had to trust that things were happening for a reason.

## 19

## JACOB

I woke up alone again for the third day in a row. I wasn't sure what the hell had happened that had scared Erin off in the middle of the night, but whatever it had been, she wasn't taking my calls and hadn't come by the office like she said she would. She had sent me one abrupt text with some lame excuse about not being able to come by to work on the project because she had things to do.

It pissed me off and hurt my feelings. I thought we had turned a corner, that we were embarking on a new beginning to our relationship. Clearly, I had been wrong. Getting blown off left me in a sour mood. I had worked on the project myself, making phone calls and trying to get a venue lined up. It wasn't easy. The moment I gave my name or the name of the company, people were booked up or busy for the weekend.

I had put all my anger and frustration squarely on Philip's shoulders. I knew Erin felt something for me. I could feel it inside her. I saw it in the way she looked at me. She wanted me as much as I wanted her. We were adults, fully capable of making our own damn decisions, but I knew her brother and father still had some pull over her. There was only one way I was going to be able to make any headway with her and that was to get all the shit out in the open.

Philip could be pissed at me. I didn't care anymore. So, what, I fell in love with his little sister and we had sex. Big fucking deal. She was eighteen and capable of making her own decisions. God knew he'd been fucking around with a number of little sisters for years. Half the women in the world were probably someone's little sister. He needed to get over himself, and I planned on telling him just that.

But first, I was going to start with Arthur. Erin had said he'd softened up a little. If I could get Arthur to accept me, it would be a hell of a lot easier to convince Philip I was worthy of dating Erin. I was a man, and I was going to have a man-to-man talk with Arthur. He was the one who had run me out of town and made some pretty serious threats. I wanted to make sure he understood I wasn't afraid of him, especially now that he wasn't wielding a badge. There was nothing he could to do to me.

It was a Saturday morning, and I was hoping the old sheriff was at home. There was no time like the present to start working on my way back into Erin's life. I wasn't a dirty little secret anymore. She could be proud of who I was and shout about our relationship from the damn rooftops.

I remembered exactly where the house was. I had spent a lot of time there during my youth and after high school. I smiled as I drove past the empty lot where I used to pick up Erin after she snuck out. Old Arthur thought he was so smart, but Erin and I had still found a way to be together.

I immediately recognized Erin's car in the driveway. Good. I wanted to talk with both of them. I didn't mind telling Erin what I wanted in front of her father. It would kill two birds with one stone. I was going to need to save my energy to take on Philip. He was going to prove to be more difficult.

I parked my truck alongside the curb and headed up the walk, taking in the few changes, including the fresh paint on the house. It was neat and tidy, just like I remembered. I took a deep breath, steeling myself for some angry words and dirty looks from the old man. I knocked on the door and waited, giving myself a silent pep talk.

"Jacob," Arthur said looking at me with surprise.

"Hello."

"What are you doing here?" Arthur asked, looking a little uncomfortable.

Good. I wanted him uncomfortable. I wanted him to have to look me in the eyes and face me as the man I was and not the scared kid I had been. I wasn't so easily intimidated. "I wanted to talk. Do you have a minute?"

"Talk?" Arthur asked, clearly stalling.

"Yes. I want to clear the air. I want to talk about what happened eight years ago and what I hope will happen in the future. I think there's a lot that was left unsaid. I want to get that all out of the way so we can all move forward," I said, keeping my voice steady.

Arthur looked behind him before looking back at me. I sensed resignation, like he might as well get it over with. That gave me confidence. He *had* softened a little over the years. Eight years ago, he would have slammed the door in my face. It was

137

progress. He stepped aside, opening the door wider and gesturing for me to go inside. I stepped through the door, figuring I better talk fast if I wanted to get out what I had to say.

"Jacob," Arthur started, and I cut him off. I knew I only had about a minute before he told me to get lost.

"Arthur—Mr. Maxwell—I know things weren't great between us in the past. There was a lot of hostility on both sides, but I'm really hoping we can leave that behind us. I am back in town, and I don't want to live in the past. I was young and dumb and did some stuff I wasn't proud of, but maybe we could find a way to move past that," I said, trying to sound reasonable.

Arthur was nodding his head. "We'll have to figure something out I suppose," he said, rounding the corner and heading for what I knew was the dining room in kitchen area. "I promise, I've changed. I've grown—" I stopped talking when I saw the same little girl from the ice cream shop sitting at the table.

I looked at Arthur, wondering why in the hell the Welsh kid was at his house. Erin appeared from the kitchen, carrying a plate with a sandwich cut in half on it. She froze when she saw me, sheer terror on her face as she looked from me to her father, silently accusing him with her eyes.

It wasn't exactly the reaction I was expecting. I had thought we had a good time the other night. I knew she enjoyed herself. I was ready to plead with her to let me take her to dinner for a real date, but the look on her face told me I was the very last person she wanted to see. "Hi," I said, hoping to diffuse whatever it was that was happening just then.

Erin stood staring at me, frozen with the plate still in her hand. "Jacob," she whispered. "You're here."

I nodded. "I am."

I looked at Arthur, who had that same expression on his face, the face that said, "Oh shit." They were both acting like I had just caught them committing a crime. *What the hell had I walked into?*

The little girl turned around and looked at me, a smile spreading across her face. "Hi," she said before looking up at Erin. "I'm hungry. Can I have my sandwich, Mommy?" the little girl asked.

Erin's eyes were locked with mine before she nodded and put the plate down in front of the child. *Mommy? Erin was a mom?* I should have seen the resemblance earlier, I supposed.

Arthur cleared his throat. "Jacob's here," he announced as if that were needed. I was pretty sure that had been established, but his comment only furthered my belief I had walked in on something I wasn't supposed to.

"I see that," Erin whispered, her face paling considerably.

The little girl sat in one of the chairs at the table, swinging her legs back and forth as she took a bite of the sandwich, clearly oblivious to the atmosphere in the room. Arthur stepped back, standing against the wall of the dining room as if he were a referee.

"We were just sitting down to lunch," Arthur said, his voice tight as he looked at me, then Erin.

"I see. I'm sorry, I didn't mean to interrupt," I mumbled, my eyes going back to the little girl.

She looked back at me. "We're having tuna fish. Do you like tuna?"

I nodded. "I do."

"My mom puts pickles in it. Mackenzie doesn't like it with pickles, but I do."

"Me too," I agreed, offering her a smile.

I guessed she must be about seven years old and very smart. I couldn't believe Erin had a kid. She never mentioned the little girl was hers. I had made the assumption she was a Welsh kid or a friend of the family. I was disappointed she hadn't told me herself but assumed she was probably embarrassed by the situation. She certainly wouldn't be the first single mom on the planet.

Hurt and jealousy were creating a fiery pit in my belly as I accepted the fact she was a mother. She had a child. There was only one way that happened. I knew it had been naïve to think she would have remained celibate after I left, but a part of me liked to think that. It made it easier to get through the days to think of her living like a nun. I couldn't stand to think of another man touching her and chose to believe it never happened.

I took a deep breath, realizing I was staring and being rude. A kid shouldn't change how I felt about her. She was still the woman I loved. I couldn't blame—

My eyes darted back to the little girl. A flurry of clips and vignettes from the encounter at the ice cream shop flashed before my eyes. My hazel eyes. The little girl had hazel eyes. I stared at the profile until the girl turned and looked at me. I took a step back, realization slamming into me like a powerful force. My mouth dropped open before I turned to look at Erin, waiting for her to tell me I wasn't looking at *my* little girl.

Erin's face was contorted with guilt. She looked away, unable to look me directly in the eyes. I turned to look at Arthur. His solemn expression also filled with guilt confirmed my suspicion. Erin had been keeping one hell of a secret from me. I felt numb. My legs felt heavy, but numb, like they were disconnected from my brain. I didn't know what to say or think. I was just dumbfounded. My mouth opened and closed as I took in the sight of the girl, happily eating a tuna fish sandwich as if nothing had changed.

But it had. My entire world had changed in an instant. I could actually feel the world tilting on its axis and spinning. *Holy shit.*

They were the only words I could think. Holy shit. A daughter. Erin had been pregnant. She had a baby. A baby that was now a kid, walking, talking, and with a vibrant personality.

I was a father.

# 20

# ERIN

I had heard the term about a person's life flashing before their eyes but had never fully understood what it meant until that very moment. I knew I wasn't facing uncertain death, but judging by the look on Jacob's face, I was facing the possibility of losing a man I loved. I couldn't believe he was standing in my father's house. I figured I would be safe at my dad's, which was why I had taken the day off and come to hang out with him. I had been worried Jacob might show up at the Welsh place to try and talk.

I never expected him to show up at my dad's, and I certainly hadn't expected my dad to invite him in. It was like I had been sucked into some alternate universe and nothing made sense. I looked at my dad, silently begging for help. He was partially to blame for the mess I was in.

"Jacob, why don't you have a seat?" he said.

My eyes widened. That was not the help I was looking for. Jacob was stiff was he pulled out one of the chairs and sat opposite Ellie, staring at her while she ate.

"Ellie, why don't we go see if that paint is dry on the birdhouse," he said.

"I'm not finished eating, Grandpa," she protested.

"You can take it with you," I said.

She frowned, clearly not happy with the suggestion, but did as she was told. She grabbed the other half of the sandwich and stomped through the kitchen and out to the garage. I took the seat Ellie vacated, folding my hands on the table and looking at Jacob.

He said nothing. He wouldn't look at me. There were so many things I wanted to say but didn't know how to actually get the words out. I could see the hurt and anger and knew I had screwed up. Fate wasn't on my side this time. I opened my mouth to say I was sorry but realized just how weak that would have sounded. Sorry wasn't quite enough to fix the situation.

He finally looked up at me. "Would you have ever told me?"

"Yes," I answered.

"When? How long were you going to keep this secret?" he asked, his voice low and gravelly, revealing his pain and anger.

"I don't know," I confessed. "I didn't know if I would ever see you again. When I found out I was pregnant, I did try and find you, but I had no idea where to look. You vanished off the face of the earth. You deactivated your Facebook; your cell phone was off. I had no idea how to find you and tell you."

"And now? I've been back for over two weeks," he reminded me.

"I didn't know if you were here to stay. I didn't know if you were just blowing through town and would up and leave like you did before."

He glared at me. "Don't you dare put that on me."

I held up a hand. "I know. I didn't mean it like that."

"A daughter. You had my baby. A baby I didn't get to see grow up. I didn't get to see her first smile or steps or say her first words. Why would do you that to me?" he asked, the words infused with anger.

My hackles went up. "Do it to you? Really, Jacob? I was the eighteen-year-old girl alone and pregnant with no job, no boyfriend, and a very angry father. I asked everyone who knew you where you went. You could have reached out. You could have stood up to my dad and tried to talk to me. You left me! Don't you dare put all of that on me! I know what they said, but I also know you! You are so much stronger than that. You could have tried harder!"

"So I could go to jail on some bullshit charge your dad made up? I don't think so. They made it clear I would never be allowed to see you. You knew the trouble it would cause if we got together, but that didn't stop you from chasing me!" he seethed.

My mouth dropped open. "You ass! You were into me just as much as I was into you."

"I told you it was wrong. I told you it would ruin my friendship with Philip. I was weak. I caved. I couldn't deny you. You should have left it be, Erin! Now I find out you had my child and didn't even bother telling me," he said, shaking his head with disgust.

I glared at him, just as pissed as he was. "I'm sorry, between being eighteen, a child myself, trying to go to college classes and raising a baby on my own, I didn't have a lot of extra time to launch a manhunt. I guess you should have thought about the possible consequences to those nights out. You were the older one. You should have known better," I spat, repeating the same thing my father had told me about the situation.

He raised an eyebrow. "You were there too. You could have said something."

I waved a hand through the air, dismissing the whole idea. "It doesn't matter. That isn't the point anyway. I love Ellie. I would never change a thing that happened."

"You see, that's the thing, you know our daughter's name. I didn't even know her name until two minutes ago. We've spent time together. You don't think you could have mentioned her then? How about when I told you I wanted to be with you, that I had never stopped caring about you? You don't think you should have said, 'Oh, hey, by the way, we have a little girl together,'" he snarled.

"It wasn't that easy," I argued.

"Really? You seem to be able to speak pretty freely when you want to. I don't get it. What was your endgame here? Is this some kind of revenge?" he asked.

"Revenge? Revenge for what?" I asked.

"You were mad I left, mad I didn't take you with me, so your way of getting back at me was to have my child and never say a word about it. Were you going to let me live here and have my daughter right under my nose and never tell me? What kind of shit is that? I thought I knew you. You are not the woman I thought you were. You're cruel and vindictive, two things I never would have expected from you," he said, getting to his feet.

"Cruel and vindictive? Not even close. I wanted to tell you. I did, but I didn't know how. I was afraid you would turn tail and run. I couldn't do that to Ellie. I couldn't tell her she had a father only to have her father abandon her," I told him, getting up and following him into the living room.

He scoffed, turning to look at me with disgust on his face. "That's bullshit and you know it. I would never do that."

"How would I know that? I haven't seen you in eight years!" I shouted before remembering Ellie and my dad weren't more than twenty feet away.

"And we both know why that is. Your dad got to raise my daughter. I'm sure Philip is the doting uncle. They made sure I wasn't around. They cut me out of my child's life. If you're pissed at anyone, be pissed at them. They did this and you let them. You went along with it, and I'm not talking about back then. I'm talking about right now. You let me talk to her at the ice cream shop. Did that make you feel good, Erin? You sat there while I looked my daughter in the eyes and said nothing. It's unforgiveable," he said before walking out the door, not bothering to close it behind him.

I followed him out to the end of the walk. "Jacob, we need to talk about this."

He stopped and looked at me over the hood of his truck

with such anger I actually shirked away. "I think it's a little late for that."

He got in his truck and sped away. I stood there for several seconds before rushing back inside and heading for the bathroom. I closed the door behind me before turning on the faucet and flushing the toilet. I wanted to drown out my sobs. I couldn't let Ellie hear me crying in the bathroom. I let myself cry for several minutes before washing my face and patting it dry.

"Oh Erin, you really did it now," I whispered, staring at my puffy red eyes in the mirror.

I had this stupid idea we could work through it. I had expected some anger and resentment, but then I thought he would forgive me, and we could move on. But he hated me. The look in his eyes as the evidence of my betrayal stared him in the face had physically hurt me to see. I couldn't imagine the pain he was feeling. I had never wanted to cause him pain or grief.

I wasn't sure if we would ever be able to make things right between us. Nothing would ever be the same again. I had ripped his heart out, and I didn't see a way for him to ever forgive me. I wasn't sure what it meant for our future. Would he want to be a part of Ellie's life? Would he give up the job he'd been working so hard to save and run away just to get some distance between us?

I shook my head. I had no idea what he would do. I had never seen him like that. The fear of the unknown had me breaking down into tears all over again. I flushed the toilet a couple more times before I managed to pull myself together and return to the kitchen. The tuna was still sitting in a bowl on the counter. The sight of it made me ill. I quickly covered it and stuck it in the fridge before cleaning up the rest of the mess.

I walked into the garage and found Ellie and my dad carefully painting the trim on the bird apartment complex. My dad's eyes met mine and I could see he was apologetic. I didn't want to hear it just then.

"Ellie, it's time to go," I said, my throat raw from the sobbing.

"Don't go," my dad said, looking at me.

I shook my head. "I need to go," I said firmly.

He sighed and nodded before walking to me and pulling me in for a hug. "For what it's worth, I am sorry for my actions back then, but I think when Ellie gets a little older, you might one day understand."

I pulled away from him. "I doubt that because I trust my daughter. I know I've raised her right, and she can make her own decisions."

"I did my best with you," he replied.

"Maybe you did, but we can't change what happened, can we? I get to live with it," I told him.

Ellie didn't look happy to be leaving her project, but she followed me anyway.

"I love you," my dad called out as I headed out the door.

I took a breath through my nose, having a very good, personal understanding about how a person could be in your life one minute and gone the next. I wasn't Philip. I didn't do grudges. I turned around and looked at my dad, seeing the sadness in his eyes. "I love you too, but right now, I don't want to be here."

He nodded. "I understand."

Ellie waved goodbye and got into the car. I turned back to make sure she was buckled and saw what Jacob would have seen—his eyes staring back at him. That realization had to have been a huge blow. He deserved to be angry. I would let him have the anger and try to talk to him once he cooled off.

## 21

## JACOB

It had been a week, and I was still struggling to get my head around the idea of being a father. Every day that passed, I kept thinking I was losing more time with a little girl who didn't even know I existed. I knew what I had to do, but I couldn't bring myself to do it just yet. My head was a mess. None of my thoughts seemed to flow coherently, and my work was suffering because of it. If I didn't pull my shit together and fast, I wasn't going to have to worry about trying to save my job because my ass was going to be fired before Western Energies could even get off the ground.

I glanced at the notes and various printouts I had collected for the ice cream social. I hadn't even been able to think about that damn thing. Every time I looked at her neat handwriting on the page, the feeling of being stabbed in the heart bubbled to the surface. I was likely feeling extra emotional due to my lack of sleep. Sleep had been a joke; every time I closed my eyes, I either thought about making love to Erin or I thought about her betrayal. Either option left me sleepless and spending the night tossing and turning. I looked rough. That's what Larry had said when I came in to work today. It wasn't a surprise. I had given up shaving a couple of days ago, and the bags under my eyes were drooping low, reminding me a lot of Droopy, one of my favorite cartoons from about a million years ago.

I wasn't going to spend another sleepless night. I was going to drink my sorrows away and hopefully knock myself out. A few stiff drinks were exactly what I needed to dull the pain enough for me to get some sleep as well as much-needed peace from my thoughts. I checked the time, figured it was after five somewhere, and called it a day.

I was going to get shitfaced. That was my goal. I didn't care that I would be drinking alone. I did a quick search to find the local cab company, which was really just a dude who had a few cars and worked from home. I didn't care. I needed a ride. I drove to my rented house and waited for the cab to swing by and pick me up.

The four-door sedan pulled up to the curb. I hopped in the front seat and asked to be taken to the Old Flame Saloon. I was hoping Erin wasn't there. I didn't want to see her, but I wanted to get liquored up and I didn't want to do it sitting alone in my house. I wanted the noise and distraction of a lively bar to help drown out the thoughts.

I walked in and took myself right up to the bar, pulling up a seat and planting my ass, ready to get started on my night of drinking.

"What's your poison?" a woman asked, sauntering over to me.

I looked at the woman with the striking green eyes and reddish-brown hair pulled back from her face. She was pretty, and maybe with a few more drinks, I might feel like flirting with her, but just then, I wasn't in the mood. Erin was still heavy on my heart and mind.

"Whiskey. Double shot," I said.

She raised her eyebrows. "Now that's a man-sized drink."

I didn't answer. I watched as she poured the drink before sliding the glass to me. I picked it up and downed it with one quick gulp. I slid the glass back toward her. "Another. Please."

She stared at me before grabbing the bottle and refilling the glass. "Maybe you want to take this one a little slower."

"I don't."

She pushed the glass toward me. I did the same thing, letting the whiskey slide down my throat, burning a trail all the way down to my gut. Without a word, I pushed the glass back to her. She let out a long sigh, slowly shaking her head as she refilled my glass.

"Whiskey doesn't drown the demons," she said in a solemn tone.

"We're going to find out," I retorted. It was then I realized she was very familiar. "I know you," I said, trying to place her.

She nodded. "Probably."

Then it hit me. "You're Erin's friend."

She winced. "Guilty as charged. Marianne Wilson, and you're Jacob Miner."

"Damn right you're guilty. I suppose you knew as well. I'm sure the whole fucking town knows," I growled.

She looked properly guilty. "It wasn't our business to say anything. This is between you and Erin."

I scoffed. "Apparently not. It was between Erin and everyone except for me—the father of the child."

"Look, I'm sorry things are strained, but there's nothing you're going to say that is going to get me switching sides. I'm Team Erin all the way. She has her reasons. I'm not saying I know all of them, but I do know she was a young girl left to raise a baby on her own," she said pointedly. "The father of her child took off and never looked back."

"I was looking back the whole damn time," I snapped.

"Were you?" she questioned, obviously not believing me.

I nodded. "I was. I was working on a plan to come back and sweep her off her feet and give her the life she deserved. I had no idea she was raising my child. A child I don't even know."

Marianne shrugged a shoulder. "I don't know what to say. There were mistakes made on both sides. Shit happens. It's what you do from here that really counts."

I looked into those green eyes that vaguely reminded me of a cat. "I guess that's easy to say when you're not the one who missed out on eight years with a woman he loved and his child."

"It isn't easy, but it's the truth."

"You don't have a child out there that you missed watching grow up."

153

Marianne reached for the bottle of whiskey and plopped it down in front of me. "You're right. On the house," she said and walked away.

I stared at the back of her head, watching as she interacted with other customers. My eyes moved around the bar that was slowly beginning to fill up with people getting off work and in need of a stiff drink. I refilled my glass and sipped the whiskey. I wasn't completely numb, but the first two drinks had taken the edge off.

I wondered how many of the people in the bar knew who I was. Then, I wondered how many of them thought I was a world-class asshole for running off after knocking up the little princess of Burning Butte. The revelation I had a kid certainly explained some of the dirty looks I had been getting since I had come back to town. I didn't know if they were aware of the full story, but I didn't see a point in trying to explain myself either. It was nobody's business. Hell, apparently it wasn't my business either. I was just the sperm donor.

I finished the third double shot and started to pour myself another, when I realized I wasn't in the mood. I was too pissed. I didn't want to end up giving some dirty looks and getting in a bar fight. There was only one person I was pissed at. I had a few things I wanted to say to Erin, and she was just going to have to sit there and listen. In my opinion, I was the wounded party in the situation. I was sick of apologizing for being run off by her damn father.

I whipped out my phone and called the cab driver and ordered a ride. I poured a single shot, slammed it down, and dropped a fifty on the counter. I wasn't a charity case. I didn't need shit on the house, especially from Team Erin.

I walked out of the bar, noticed the sun was just beginning its slow descent from the sky, and took a deep breath. The air was thick and humid, suggesting a storm was on the way in. That was perfect. I wanted something violent and loud. I wanted to hear the sky rage and protest. I wanted someone to acknowledge how I felt and just give me a minute of sympathy. I didn't need a lot, just someone to ease the ache I had been feeling since I had found out.

The cab pulled up. I got in the back seat for my second ride and ordered him to take me to the Welsh mansion. When he dropped me off at the closed gate, I realized I had a bit of a conundrum. I wasn't necessarily drunk, but I had been drinking and I was sure the whiskey was strong on my breath. I didn't want to see Larry. I wanted to see Erin. I waited until the cab pulled away before following the fence line down about thirty feet before reaching into my old box of tricks and scaling the fence. I knew it was ridiculous, but I was desperate to see her.

I walked across the manicured grounds, heading for the garage. I went around the back and looked up, seeing Erin walk past one of the windows. I waved my arms, trying to get her attention. She didn't notice me. I bent down, picked up a small pebble, and threw it at the window. It was a flashback to our youth when I had done this exact same thing on several occasions, albeit, on a ground floor window.

She came to the window and looked down. Her mouth dropped open. She quickly slid the window open and stared at me. "What the hell are you doing?"

"I want to talk to you," I answered, sounding perfectly reasonable.

"Oh my god! You're going to get us both fired."

"I'm not leaving until we talk," I told her.

She growled, mumbling something under her breath as she disappeared from the window. I stood, waiting to see what she was doing. I half expected Larry to appear and chase me off the grounds, or Philip waving his badge around.

"Dammit, Jacob, what are you doing here," I heard Erin say and spun around to see her coming out of a side door.

"I want to talk."

"I'm taking you home before someone sees you. Come on," she grumbled, snatching my hand and dragging me through the garage toward her car.

"I don't care who sees me anymore," I told her, flopping into the passenger seat of her car. "The only reason I took this stupid job was to come back for you. It doesn't matter anymore. The secret you kept from me changes everything. Nothing is the same."

Erin was quiet as she pulled out of the Welsh driveway and headed down the road. "Jacob, you've been drinking. I'm not going to have this discussion with you right now."

"Yes, you are. I'm not drunk."

"Whatever," she said, shaking her head.

"Everywhere I go, I can feel people looking at me. This whole time I thought they were looking at me with anger and disgust because of the trouble I got into before I was run out of here. Now I realize they're staring at me because they know. Everyone knows! Everyone knew except for me! And they think I left because of it," I said, my voice rising.

"No one knew."

"Bullshit! You know the way people talk around here."

She sighed. "They suspected, but I have never once talked publicly about Ellie's father."

I scoffed. "As if you had to. Your dad and Philip made damn sure everyone knew how much they hated me. That bullshit started before I even left. They were already working at turning people against me before I even got a chance to defend myself. And then this. You had our child, raised her," I said, unable to keep talking. It still baffled my mind.

She was quiet, saying nothing as she drove me home. I began to wonder if she had anything *to* say. I didn't know what she *could* say that would make any of it any better.

## 22

### ERIN

I parked my car in his driveway alongside his truck. I was thankful he had been smart enough not to get behind the wheel. I turned off the car and looked at him. He was glowering at me. "I'll walk you in," I said in a soft voice.

"We're going to talk," he said, determination in his tone.

I nodded, grateful that Ellie was having another "sleep over" in Mackenzie's room. "We'll talk, after you've had some coffee."

He threw open the car door, stomping up the walk and fumbling with his keys until he managed to get the door open. I followed behind him, knowing he had a right to be upset, but hoped he could have a rational conversation. Our last one hadn't gone so well.

It didn't take me long to find the K-Cups for the coffee machine. I quickly made him a cup, not really thrilled to be drinking coffee after eight, but figured I may as well. I could be up for a while. I wanted to talk through the situation, and hopefully the two of us could come to some kind of under-standing. We had a child to think about and couldn't let our feelings get in the way.

Jacob had stomped into his bedroom the moment we had come through the door. I hoped he hadn't passed out. He was the one who demanded we talk. I picked up both cups of coffee just as he was coming down the hall wearing nothing but a pair of sweats slung low on his hips. He looked dangerous. The scruff on his face combined with his hair that was just a touch longer than he usually kept it gave him an edgy look. In his youth, he'd had that same edge, but it looked far darker and a hell of a lot sexier now than it had back then.

"Here," I said, holding out the cup of coffee.

"I'm not drunk," he protested.

"Fine, but you've been drinking."

"I needed to."

I followed him to the couch, sitting on the far end. It was hard to be near him and not touch him, especially looking the way he did. I had thought I was over the bad-boy thing, but hot damn, seeing him like that was making me all warm and squishy inside.

"Thank you for being willing to talk about this. I know it's been tough for you. It's been hard for me as well," I told him.

He gave me a dirty look. "Really? What part was hard? The part where your secret was exposed?"

I took a deep breath. Clearly, he was still angry. "I don't like keeping secrets."

"Your actions would say otherwise."

"I deserve that and I'm sorry. I never intended for it to be a secret. It was just a shock. You showed up at the door, and I had no idea how to tell you. I didn't know you were going to be sticking around. Then it always felt like the wrong time. I didn't know how to tell you. I knew you were going to be hurt and angry, and to be honest, I didn't want that," I confessed.

"Oh no, we wouldn't want me to be mad or hurt, so let's keep the fact I fathered a child a secret for another eight years," he grumbled.

"Jacob, I wanted to tell you. I did, but it just, I don't know," I said, frustrated by the lack of progress in getting past the situation.

"You certainly didn't try very hard. I would think it would be fairly simple. Something like, 'by the way, you have a little girl,' or something along those lines. It couldn't have been all that difficult. I think it's because you liked your little secret. It gave you power," he sneered.

I had had enough. I leaned forward and put my coffee cup on the coffee table before getting to my feet. "Clearly, you didn't want to talk. You wanted to bitch at me and try to make me feel worse than I already do. I'm not here for you to berate me. I'm here to have a real conversation. Maybe when you sober up, that can happen."

I walked to the door but didn't get a chance to open it. He grabbed my arm, spinning me around and crowding against me with his bare chest. I stepped back, my back coming up against the wall. I stared into his eyes filled with anger.

"I'm perfectly sober," he hissed, the sweet smell of whiskey clouding the air I was breathing.

"Whatever. Let go of me. I don't have to listen to you. You have no idea what it was like for me. No idea what I felt," I snapped.

His lip curled. "You have no idea how *I* felt. I never stopped thinking about that first night together. The night I took your virginity. I claimed you. No other man had touched you. I was intent on being the last. You were the one for me. I always intended to come back for you. Everything I have done these past eight years was with the goal of coming back here. I fought hard, I worked harder, and I did it all because I wanted to be here with you."

"Jacob, I didn't know! How could I have known? Eight years! Do you know how long that is? People get married and divorced in that time!" I argued, beyond frustrated with him and the situation as a whole.

"I know exactly how long it is! It was seven birthdays I missed out on with my little girl. Thousands of days and nights without you in my arms. Milestones and memories were all missed out on because I couldn't be here. I kept telling myself it would be worth it. I would get into a position where I could come back and sweep you off your feet, give you the life you deserved, and be able to tell your dad and brother to fuck off because I could take care of you far better than they could!" he said, his voice loud, the anger making a muscle twitch in the corner of his eye.

I sighed. He had lost a lot. "I'm sorry. My god, I'm so sorry.

NATASHA L. BLACK

I've told you I'm sorry over and over. I don't know what else to say. I don't know what you want me to do to make it better. You're right. You did lose out on precious time. We have to move forward. What's done is done," I insisted. "How can we move forward?" His eyes bored into mine. I felt like he was scanning my brain, looking into my very soul. His gaze dropped, looking at my mouth and making me feel flushed. A wave of heat washed over my body. I knew what he was thinking. I slowly shook my head until his gaze met mine again.

"I want what I worked so hard for. I want what I'm afraid I'll never have to call my own," he whispered.

I tried to push away from him, but his body moved closer, his chest pushed against mine. He reached out and grabbed my wrist, his fingers encircling it and lifting my arm, pinning my arm to the wall beside my head. I wasn't afraid, but I was worried about his state of mind.

"Jacob." I breathed his name in an attempt to stop him.

His mouth closed over mine as he held my head against the wall. He reached and grabbed my free hand with his other hand, both of my arms now pinned against the wall with his body pushed against mine, his mouth holding mine hostage. I tried to tell him we shouldn't, but his tongue plunged deep inside, blocking the words from ever leaving my mouth.

I arched my back, attempting to push him away from me, which only served to press my breasts against him. I gasped as a jolt of desire rocked my body. He was different, aggressive and turning me on. I quit trying to push him away and gave in to the desire. Somewhere in the back of my mind I told myself one more time wouldn't hurt.

He must have felt the change and took his kiss up another notch, moving his mouth to my jaw and down my neck. He sucked large swaths of skin between his teeth, biting my neck like he was a vampire in search of the right vein. I moaned, crying out in pain and pleasure. I moved my lower body, rubbing myself against the erection I could feel through the sweats he was wearing.

"God, I want you. I fucking *need* you," he growled next to my ear, sucking my earlobe between his teeth before returning to my neck that was now damp with his kisses.

"I'm here, I'm here," I gasped, my heart racing and my own need ramping up with every kiss.

He let go of my wrists, jerking at the waistband of the jean shorts I had on. He quickly flicked the button open, jerked the zipper down, and pushed the shorts down my legs with one forceful move.

My shorts anchored around my ankles. With his lower body still pressed against mine, I was helpless to try and kick them off. He was all hands and mouth, moving with such intensity I could barely catch my breath. I kept my arms up against the wall, unsure of what else to do with them. I felt a hard tug and heard a faint tear and realized he'd torn my lace panties from my body.

"Jacob," I panted, feeling like I was caught up on a speeding train with no way off. Hell, I didn't think I wanted off.

"Turn around," he barked.

I couldn't move. He stepped back and grabbed my shoulder, turning me around before pushing me forward. I turned my face, my cheek resting against the wall. The man was feral. I hated to admit it to myself, but I liked it. I liked seeing him unhinged. I liked knowing he was that way for me. I could feel him jerking his pants down, his knuckles scraping over my skin as he did, one hand still pushed against me, holding me against the wall. I protested his hand against me and jerked my shoulders.

"Don't fucking move," he growled, using his forearm across my back to hold me still.

His other hand moved between my thighs, pushing my legs apart. I didn't get a chance to ready myself for his intrusion. He was pushing inside me before I could protest again.

I shouted, slapping my hand against the wall as he drove himself inside me. It was only because I wanted him so much that he was able to slide inside my body with one hard thrust. He grunted, driving against me again and again. There was no mercy in each one of his thrusts. It was angry and passionate and the hottest, most erotic thing I had ever experienced in my life. I pushed back, using my hand to leverage myself away from the wall, and slammed my back into his chest.

He roared, pushing me back in place, one hand dropping to my hip as he held me up against the wall, taking everything he wanted from me. I dug my nails into the wall, the ecstasy of the moment making my legs weak. His firm hand on my hip and the other pinning me against the wall were the only things keeping me vertical. His impassioned groans and grunts were raking over my senses, taking me closer to an orgasm I knew was going to be powerful and violent.

I braced myself against the wall, both hands at head level,

my fingers digging in as if I were climbing a steep cliff. His body bounced against mine, my breasts rubbing against the wall with every thrust. The friction of my nipples against the wall teased me higher and higher until I was absolutely convinced I would shatter into a million pieces.

## 23

## JACOB

I couldn't stop myself. She was everything I couldn't have. She was everything I wanted. My body was out of control as I buried myself deep inside her, jerking and grunting like a raging beast. It wasn't enough. I was furious with her and wanted her at the same time.

"Jacob!" she cried out my name, her voice full of lust.

I moved faster; my thrusts more purposeful. It was like being on a speeding train. I couldn't have gotten off the ride if I wanted to, not until I reached my destination.

"Stop talking," I ordered, the intensity of my thrusts bouncing her against the wall, vibrating the picture hanging a few feet away.

I felt a gush of warmth and knew she had orgasmed. It drove me harder. My fingers dug into her flesh, yanking her hips back and against me as I met them with deep strokes. The orgasm was hovering just out of reach. I pulled back, using one hand to force her down, bending her over as her hands clung to the wall for support. The new position allowed me to go deeper as I took her hard and fast. The word *more* echoed through my mind. I wanted more. I wanted it all. I didn't want to stop until I had gotten my fill.

The sound of her whimpers and moans and our bodies slapping together in the dim living room echoed around me. I could hear my own heavy breathing as I kept up the furious pace. In a flash, it was too much. A nerve was tweaked, and before I could stop it from happening, I was exploding deep inside her. I roared with a fierce victory cry as if I had won the battle waging inside me.

When I was completely spent, I stepped away from her, yanking up my sweats. I felt a little guilty for the rough sex and felt I should apologize. I watched as Erin stood, pulling up her shorts and quickly fastening them before turning to look at me. "I should go," she muttered.

"Of course," I smirked.

"Dammit, Jacob. Why do you do this? We can't have a simple conversation without it leading to sex," she snapped.

I raised an eyebrow. "We've had plenty of conversations without having sex. I'll admit I'm usually thinking about sex the entire time though," I said with a grin, knowing it would piss her off.

"It isn't funny! We can't let our physical attraction for one another cloud our judgment. We have to be able to talk and work through things," she argued with exasperation. She put one hand on her hip and stared at me.

All I could think about was the fact she didn't have any panties on. They were sitting right on the floor beside her. Her lips were red and swollen, and her hair was a mess. She had the look of a woman who'd just had a very good time, and I wanted her again. She'd probably kill me if she knew just how much I wanted to cloud the conversation again.

"What you really mean is you want to slink out of here and get back home before anyone realizes you've been out catting around," I said with a vicious smile.

Her mouth dropped open. "I brought you home because you were drunk!"

"I'm not drunk. I wasn't drunk," I argued.

"Whatever!"

"Go ahead, crawl on out of here. That's what you do. I'm just another one of your dirty little secrets. You don't want anyone to know I still get you off. You don't want anyone to think the town princess is laying with the guy from the wrong side of town. I get it, go ahead," I said, shooing her out the door.

The look of anger on her face had me wanting her all over again. "You're such an asshole! Stay away from me!" she growled and yanked open the front door.

"Don't run out," I said in a low voice.

She stopped and turned around, looking me in the eyes, anger flashing through hers. "You said you wanted to talk. I wanted to talk. I wanted to work through this."

"Work through this? This being the fact you kept my child from me, and even after having ample opportunity to tell me about her, you didn't? Is that the 'this' you're speaking of, because if it is, all the talking in the world isn't going to make it better. It isn't going to change the fact you lied to me over and over and then had the audacity to try and blame me for not knowing. News flash, Erin: a man doesn't immediately know when he's impregnated a woman," I told her.

"I know that, but I've explained why I didn't tell you, why I couldn't tell you. This situation is unfortunate, but it doesn't mean we have to hate each other. There is a child involved. Can't you get over yourself long enough to think about her?" she said in a tone that sounded very condescending to me.

I smirked. "Odd that you say that because that's exactly what I was going to say to you."

Her mouth opened and shut before she pursed her lips together. "This is getting us nowhere. You're still angry and being unreasonable. I'm not about to stand here and waste my time with you."

"You didn't mind standing right up against the wall while I was buried inside you. I guess that's different though. You felt good when I was inside you. That's what you like about me. That's all I'm good for, right?" I hissed.

"No," she whispered. "That's not true. You know it isn't like that."

I shook my head. "I don't know. You would have kept on fucking me without ever mentioning the kid. You liked what I could do for you, but I wasn't good enough to be told I was a father. You're just like the rest of them."

"No, I'm not! I've said I was sorry. I've tried to explain what happened. I know I screwed up, and I feel terrible about it, but this isn't helping. We're only going to say things we end up regretting," she said, her voice soft, her eyes pleading.

I stared back at her. "I regret nothing I've said."

She shook her head. "This isn't you. This isn't who you are. This is the whiskey and hurt talking."

I smirked, folding my arms across my chest. "This is me. This is the man your daddy didn't want you to have anything to do with. I'm the man who made a baby with you, but since your daddy said I wasn't good enough, you believed him. You kept her from me."

"Enough. I'm done," she said, turning to walk out the door.

I watched as she slammed it behind her. A flash of white caught my eye, and I couldn't resist. I bent down and snatched the torn panties and walked to the door, pulling it open. "You forgot your panties," I shouted loud enough for the entire neighborhood to hear.

I heard her growl, but she kept walking. I stood in the doorway, watching her back out of the driveway and leave. It was then that it all hit me. "Fuck," I said with a sigh, closing the door and locking it.

That was not how I wanted things to go. I had lashed out at the person I felt had hurt me. I turned off the few lights and headed for bed. I lay there staring up at the dark ceiling and wondering what the hell I had done. I just seemed to be making things worse. I sure as hell didn't feel any better after the way I had spoken to her.

I was so angry. So hurt. I couldn't get over the idea I had lost out on so much. I felt like I had been robbed of precious time and memories. There weren't enough ways to say sorry to make up for that. Despite the anger and pain I felt, I knew it would only get worse. The anger would sour my life if I let it. I had worked too damn hard to pull myself up from nowhere to let something like this destroy everything.

I had two choices. I could choose to wallow in the grief or put it aside and focus on making the future special. I had a little girl who still didn't know who I was. It had been a week. I had lost out on another week because I'd been letting my hurt get in the way. I closed my eyes, imagining what it would be like to be a father.

"Oh shit," I whispered, my eyes popping open.

A father provided for his child. Erin had argued she'd struggled being a teenager raising a baby. Had my little girl suffered? Had she been lacking because I was absent? Guilt slammed into me. I thought about Erin and how young and innocent she had been. The idea of her becoming a mom shortly after I left was hard to accept. I knew there was no way Arthur would have ever let Erin or her daughter go without, but it should have been my responsibility.

I should have been around to make sure she had food to eat and a roof over her head. Erin had to give up all her dreams to take care of our child. A child who didn't get the benefit of having her father in her life. Guilt flayed me, slicing me open and making me feel like the worst human on the planet. I had been so caught up in how bad I felt, I didn't stop to think about the little girl—Ellie. Erin had said she didn't want to tell me initially because she was protecting our daughter's feelings. She was right to do so. I was glad she had tried to feel me out first. It gave me a modicum of comfort to know she had our daughter's best interests at heart.

It was time to set aside my pain and anger and put Ellie's needs first. I had a long way to go to make things right with Erin. I wasn't sure we could ever be together, but I could be there for Ellie. I could be a father. I hoped Erin wasn't so pissed at me she would try and keep me from getting to know my daughter. I didn't think she was like that, but I had been a real dick. I owed her an apology. I wasn't necessarily ready to try and make things work between us, but I wanted to be civil for our daughter's sake.

Even on my darkest days the past week, I realized the pain I felt was because I loved Erin so much, that to think of her hurting me cut me deep. The betrayal stung, but I still loved her. Relationships weren't supposed to be easy I supposed. It took work on both sides.

I closed my eyes again, feeling at peace knowing what I had to do. Now, I just had to hope I hadn't completely ruined things.

# 24

## ERIN

I tossed a load of laundry into the dryer in my apartment and hit the button. I could hear the annoying laugh of SpongeBob coming from the living room, followed by Ellie's own hysterical laughter. SpongeBob was timeless, I realized. He would be making kids laugh for many years to come. I loved our Sundays together, just hanging out the two of us. I was officially off, although it usually ended up with the kids wanting to play together in the backyard.

I heard a knock on the door, assumed it must be one of the kids asking if Ellie could play, and made my way over, the basket of laundry I needed to fold under one arm. When I opened the door, it was Ivy standing on the other side. That was unexpected. She never bothered me on a Sunday, firm in the belief I needed a full day off.

"Hi, Ivy. What's up?" I asked.

"You have a visitor," she said with a grin.

"I have a visitor?" I asked, wondering if she was referring to herself. Ivy tended to be a little eccentric at times.

She let out an exasperated sigh. "Yes. Jacob. He's now got Larry talking about business. Seriously, do they ever think of anything else?" she pouted. "I'm so sick of all work and no play. Larry never wants to do anything or go anywhere. I miss the days when we would spend time together. I don't even feel like I know him anymore."

"I'm sorry. I didn't know Jacob was coming by. Are you sure he's here for me?" I asked gently.

"Yes. He asked for you. Larry invited him into his study, and that's where they have been ever since. We were supposed to be going to a movie in Bismarck. Anything to get out of here. I'm so bored!"

I felt bad for her. I knew she had been struggling since they'd moved away from the city. She had no friends and had nothing in common with anyone around the area. Larry was her only friend, and he had all but abandoned her. "I'll get Jacob. Then, why don't I take the kids for the day and you and Larry can go watch that movie," I offered.

"No, I couldn't ask you to do that," she replied.

"Hey, it's fine. I don't mind. They'll probably end up hanging out together anyway."

She mulled it over and nodded. "Okay, fine, but I'm giving you a day off during the week," she insisted.

"Works for me," I said with a grin. "Let me put this away and I will be right down."

"Thank you, Erin. You are an absolute lifesaver and maybe even a marriage saver," she muttered, heading back down the stairs.

I put on some shoes, got Ellie off the TV, and headed downstairs. I was nervous as hell to see Jacob after last night, but it had to happen eventually. I may as well get it over with, I told myself. I took Ellie to the playroom where Mackenzie and Mitchell were in a heated game of Minecraft. I didn't want to bring Ellie to Jacob just yet. If his mood was anything like last night, I refused to let him see her. He was pissed and I got it, but he wasn't going to disrespect me or say something that might hurt her feelings. I would claw his eyes out.

"I'll be back in a bit. Maybe we can go to the park later," I told them.

There were squeals of excitement as I left the room. The kids loved the park, even though their backyard was better than any park we had in town. I went to the study first and found it empty. I searched in the living room and then went outside, spotting the men in the kitchen through the window. Seeing Jacob pulled at my heart. No matter how angry I was with him, I was drawn to him.

I opened the door and stepped inside, my eyes on Jacob, trying to gauge his mood. He looked at me and offered a small smile. "Hi," he said.

"Erin! We were just talking about the ice cream social you and Jacob have been working on. It sounds like a great idea. Do you think it will work?" he asked.

I shrugged a shoulder. "We often have big cookouts in the park for holidays or because someone has retired or is moving away. It's a good way for everyone to come together in a relaxed environment. The kids can play, and parents don't have to worry about finding babysitters. I think it will be a good way for people to see you and your family and actually talk to you instead of feeling like you aren't approachable."

Larry was nodding his head. "I think that just might work."

Ivy came into the kitchen wearing heels and a pretty summer dress with a deep V in the front showing off a healthy amount of cleavage. Larry's eyes widened and Jacob looked away. The woman certainly knew how to make an entrance.

"Let's go, Larry," she said leaving no room for argument.

Larry looked stupefied. "Go? Go where? Why are you dressed like that?"

"We're going out. Me and you. I don't care where, but you are taking me out and we will not be talking about work. I need some attention," she said boldly.

I had to hide my smile.

"But the kids," Larry said in a small voice.

"Erin's watching them. Now, Larry. I'm giving you one last chance," she snapped.

Larry looked at me. "Thank you," he said and quickly rushed to his wife's side. "You two keep up the good work. I'm anxious to hear more about this ice cream social."

"Now, Larry!" Ivy hollered, walking out of the kitchen.

Jacob turned to look at me. I could see the heavy circles under his eyes, but he had shaved this morning and looked a little better than he had last night. "What are you doing here?" I asked him.

"I came to see her."

"Ellie?" I asked suddenly nervous.

He nodded his head, making no move to step toward me. "Yes. She's my daughter. I'm hoping we can set aside our differences so that I may have a relationship with her. What's happened between us should not affect that. I want to know her."

I nodded. I wouldn't deny him that chance. "Okay."

"Okay?" he repeated, seemingly surprised by my quick agreement.

"Yes. I told the kids I would take them to the park. You're welcome to join us. It will give you a chance to hang out with Ellie without her or you feeling pressure. She's an easygoing kid, but I haven't exactly explained this situation. I'd like to ease her into the idea of having a daddy in her life," I said with a smile.

I was trying to play it cool, but inside, my heart was breaking. He had said nothing about the two of us and what our relationship might be. I had pushed him too far. He wasn't interested in me anymore. I gulped down the ball of emotion lodged in my throat and waited for his response.

After a few seconds, he nodded. "I'd like that. When?" he asked stiffly.

"How about an hour?" I offered.

"I'll grab some lunch for everyone and meet you there," he said, his tone a little chilly.

"Okay, see you then," I said, trying to keep my voice even.

He walked out of the kitchen without saying another word. I steeled my emotions. I knew it was a possibility he would want nothing to do with me now. Hell, I had been mad enough last night to feel like that, but every time I saw him, my anger diminished, and I just wanted him to hold me.

I pulled myself together and went back to tell the kids our plans. With Ivy and Larry off doing whatever, I took Mackenzie and Mitchell back up to my apartment for me to change and get ready for a day at the park. I put on a flirty, lightweight shirt, added a little mascara to my eyelashes, and called it good. I didn't want to look like I was trying too hard. I hoped he relaxed a little when we got to the park. "Okay, guys! Ready for a picnic at the park?" I shouted into the living room.

"You didn't make any sandwiches," Ellie said when I came out of the bathroom.

I smiled. "That's because my friend, Jacob, is going to be meeting us there, and he is going to bring sandwiches for everyone!"

Ellie looked skeptical. "I hope he brings tuna."

"I think there is a pretty good chance he will," I told her. "But remember, you tell him thank you regardless of what kind of sandwich he brings, right?" I said, looking at all three kids and earning silent nods.

"All right, load up," I ordered, grabbing the keys for the Welsh SUV. They preferred I used the Tahoe when I was transporting their kids. It was safer and they claimed they didn't want me wasting my gas using my personal vehicle to drive their kids around.

As I drove, I thought about the tuna fish sandwiches. I knew Jacob loved tuna. It hadn't been a surprise when I had given Ellie a tuna sandwich at three years old and she had gobbled it down. I remembered smiling and crying at the same time while she ate the sandwich. It had made me miss him even more. I had seen the look on his face when he had come to my dad's and saw her eating his favorite lunch. There were so many other little things that they shared. I couldn't wait for him to get to know her like I knew her. I wanted her to know him and understand where she came from and how much they were alike.

I knew it was going to be a long road, but I was so hoping Jacob was in for the long haul. I knew Ellie would welcome him with open arms, once we talked about who he was to her. I wasn't quite ready to drop that bombshell on her. We arrived at the park, and I thanked my lucky stars it was empty. Fortunately, the heat tended to drive everyone indoors. I didn't want anyone from town watching Jacob and Ellie together. I felt like it should be a private reunion. He had been right; everyone knew. Everyone was going to be watching how it all unfolded and judging his parenting abilities. I hated that he had to go through it and hoped he would let me be by his side as he did.

Jacob pulled in behind us, parking a few spots away from the Tahoe as if he were afraid to get to close. I unloaded the kids from the vehicle and told them to go play.

"Can I help?" I asked, seeing him reaching for several bags from one of the local restaurants.

"I got it," he grumbled.

I nodded, silently walking beside him to one of the picnic

tables under the shade of a large tree. "I'll call them over," I said, feeling the tension between us and wanting some buffers.

He nodded, unpacking the burgers and fries. I hoped Ellie wasn't too disappointed there weren't any tuna sandwiches.

## 25

### JACOB

It was kind of surreal to be sitting down to lunch with my seven-year-old daughter for the first time in both of our lives. I couldn't stop staring at her. She was a pretty little girl and looked a lot like Erin. She was giggling and talking with her friends.

I turned to find Erin watching me. I held her gaze for a few seconds before turning back to look at Ellie. The little girl looked at me and smiled. "Thank you for the burgers."

I smiled back. "You're welcome."

"I thought you were going to bring tuna. My mom always makes tuna for picnics."

I nodded. "Maybe next time," I said, making it clear there would be a next time.

"Do you want to push me on the swing?" she asked.

I chuckled and looked at the half-eaten burger in her hand. "Is that a good idea after you've eaten?"

She wrinkled her nose in a way that looked so much like Erin I was taken aback. "I think so. Why would it be a bad idea?"

I turned to Erin, who was smiling and watching. "She's got a pretty iron stomach."

"An iron stomach?" Ellie repeated.

"It means you don't get sick from spinning and swinging, stuff like that," I explained.

"I love spinning!" she exclaimed, her eyes wide.

I grinned. "So does your mom. It makes me a little queasy."

"So, can you push me?" she asked again, completely over our conversation about who could handle spinning and who couldn't.

I grabbed a napkin and wiped my hands. "I can. Let's do this."

She slid off the bench and raced across the grass to the swings. I turned back to find Erin watching us. The Welsh kids were still eating their lunch and content to stay with Erin, which left me alone with Ellie. Suddenly, I was a little freaked-out. I wasn't sure how to talk or what to say. I'd been around three kids in my lifetime, if that. I had zero experience and had no idea how hard to push her or anything.

I had to prove I was capable of being a good father. I felt like I was being interviewed for the position. She didn't even trust me enough to tell me I had a kid. Allowing said kid to spend any time with me was going to be a huge feat. I was up for the challenge. I would take classes if I had to. I was going to be a part of Ellie's life.

"Have a seat," I instructed.

She giggled. "I know, silly."

"Sorry," I muttered.

"I like to go really high. Don't push me like my mom does. She only does it a little bit," she instructed.

"I think for both our safety, I better stick to normal pushing. I don't want your mom mad at me," I told her.

She let out a long sigh. "Fine."

I grabbed the chains and pulled back before pushing her forward. I repeated the process, back and forth, adding a little more energy each time. Soon, she was soaring through the air, her hair flying out behind her as she squealed with laughter.

"Too much?" I asked her, pulling the chains and slowing her down.

"No! More!"

I chuckled and pushed her away before dancing around to stand in front of her. "Oh no! You're going to hit me!" I cried out when she started swinging forward.

She burst into laughter as I pretended to be terrified, dodging out of the way at the last second. Her laughter echoed around me as she sailed back, leaning back before pointing her pointing her feet directly at me. "I'm going to get you!"

I dropped to the ground and let her fly right over me. She was laughing so hard I feared she would fall out of the swing. I found myself laughing. Her laughter was infectious. We played the game a little longer before she grew tired of the swinging. I slowed it down and helped her off. The Welsh kids rushed over, and all three kids ran to the large jungle gym and started climbing up.

The little boy turned and pointed at me, shouting, "He's the monster! Run!"

At first, I wasn't quite sure what was happening, but when I heard the screams followed by raucous laughter, I quickly caught on. It was like being around the kids opened the memory vault. I remembered being their age. I roared, putting my hands up and making claws as I ran around the structure. More screams as I pretended to try and grab them. Ellie reminded me so much of Erin. She had that carefree smile and laugh, just like Erin. She was light on her feet and seemed to have fun no matter what the situation.

Erin had cleaned up the table and was walking toward us. She was smiling, watching the kids play before she turned to look at me. I stared at her, letting my own smile slip. I was still angry and hurt. Getting the chance to know Ellie made the pain even deeper. I had known her for ten minutes and I could see she was a great kid.

"Having fun?" Erin asked.

"Yes."

"She likes you," Erin commented.

"She should; I'm her father," I said in a low voice.

I hadn't meant to be rude, but I knew that's what it sounded like. "You're right. The two of you are a lot alike. She is a good girl, funny and kind and strong."

"She looks like you. She has many of your mannerisms. She reminds me of you when you were younger," I said, not looking at her. "I imagine she will be a beautiful young woman, which I'm not sure I like," I grumbled.

"She has your eyes," she replied.

I nodded. "She does. It's strange to think I was a part of making a little human. I never imagined someone sharing my genes."

Her warm smile nearly melted the ice had erected around my heart, but I pushed back against it. "I remember when she was born and counting all her little fingers and toes. I couldn't believe I had grown a tiny baby in my body. I wanted desperately to share that moment with you."

The ice I thought was melting spread through me. Her words were like being doused with a bucket of cold water. "I would have liked to have seen her then. I would have liked to share that moment with you."

Her eyes dropped. "I'm sorry. I truly am sorry. She's spectacular and I'm not just saying that because she's mine. She really is a good kid. I couldn't have asked for any better."

"I know I've had no part in the shaping of who she is right now, but I hope I can be a part of her future growth. I want to be a part of all of it. The tears, the discipline, the milestones, all of it, even the hard stuff. This isn't something you have to do on your own. I'm here and I'm not going anywhere," I said, staring directly into her eyes and making sure she knew I meant it.

"She's a good kid. She's has all our best qualities. Although, she has a little bit of a temper," she said with a laugh.

I winced, knowing that part had come from me. "Good. A girl needs to be strong and stubborn."

"Let's play tag!" Ellie shouted. "You're it," she said, pointing at me.

"Me?" I asked with surprise, knowing I could outrun them.

"Run!" Mitchell hollered.

The three kids jumped off the jungle gym and scattered in different directions, all of them screaming as they ran for the trees. I had my work cut out for me. I raced after Ellie first, slowing down a little so I didn't overtake her too fast. I gave chase, letting her escape my attempt to tag her several times before finally reaching out and touching her.

"You're it!" I shouted.

"I'm going to get you!" she returned.

I raced away, hiding behind a tree while she gave chase to her friend Mackenzie. We ran and played for what felt like forever until we all stopped, falling onto the grass and sucking in deep gulps of air. I was beat. It had been a long time since I had run around like that. They had endless buckets of energy. I rolled to my side to check on the kids and saw Erin sitting on a bench watching us.

The happy smile she'd had earlier was gone. She looked sad. I wasn't sure why she looked sad, but I wasn't all that concerned. If she was sad because I was enjoying myself with our daughter, too fucking bad. She had probably had countless days at the park with Ellie. This was my first; the first of many if I had anything to say about it.

"I want to go down the slide," Ellie announced.

I groaned. "Aren't you tired?" I asked her.

She jumped to her feet. "No. Are you?"

"Yes, actually I am. I'm old. I can't run as fast as you," I muttered.

Ellie moved over to stand over me. "How old are you? Are you as old as my grandpa?"

I chuckled and shook my head. "No, I'm not that old. I'm twenty-nine."

"My mom is twenty-six. She's a little bit old," she said with all the sureness of a seven-year-old.

I grinned, sitting up looking up at her. "I don't think ladies like to be called old."

"I said she's a little bit old. She's not old and wrinkly," she clarified.

I nodded. "I see. Am I old?"

She shrugged. "You're not wrinkly."

I heard Erin laugh and had to laugh myself. Only a kid could get away with such bluntness. "Let's do this slide thing. Do I catch you or what?" I asked.

She wrinkled her nose. "I'm not a baby."

"Does that mean I don't catch you?"

She rolled her eyes, sounding and looking very much like her mother. "No. Come on, I'll show you," she grumbled.

I got to my feet and walked to the slide. I could see Erin watching us. It was killing me to stay away from her. There was so much I wanted from her, for her, and to know she didn't trust me enough to be a partner in this whole parenting thing, it hurt. It made me second-guess everything.

"Okay, I'm here," I announced, holding my arms out.

"I'm coming, watch out!" Ellie cried out, coming down the slide with speed that terrified me.

My instinct was to reach out and scoop her up, which is exactly what I did. I lifted her up and carefully put her on her feet a few feet away from the slide. "Are you okay?"

She scowled. "I'm fine. You picked me up."

"You were going fast," I retorted.

"I'm a big girl," she protested.

"Ellie," Erin said in a warning voice. "Mind your manners, young lady."

"Sorry," Ellie said.

"It's fine. You are a big girl. You want to do it again? I won't catch you this time."

She sighed. "No. I'm good. I'm thirsty."

"I brought some water. Why don't we all go get a drink?" I suggested.

We all sat down at the picnic table again, rehydrating with

the cold waters. Erin took a seat beside Ellie, using one hand to brush her hair back. I watched as she smiled at our daughter, looking at her with such tenderness and love. Ellie looked up at her, smiling as she drank from her bottle. The two of them looked a lot like. I imagined Ellie would look more like Erin the older she grew.

I was more determined than ever to be a part of her life. I wasn't sure what that all entailed; if I had to get a lawyer and get a custody agreement, I would do it. I wasn't going to walk away. I would pay every penny of back child support. I would do classes, buy a house, and do whatever it took to be a permanent part of Ellie's life. I wasn't sure if Western Energies was in Burning Butte to stay, but I was. I would find another job. I would find a way to make a good living, enough to support Ellie.

I looked at Erin, letting her know just how determined I was. No one was running me out of town again, not even if they were packing heat. I had everything to lose and would not go down without a fight.

# 26

## ERIN

He was so different. I knew he had caught me staring at him several times. I couldn't help it. I kept looking at him, trying to align the man I was seeing in front of me with the guy I had known back then. He had been short-tempered, cocky, and always looking for trouble. The man today was fun and energetic and very patient. I loved the easy way he had with all of the kids. He never yelled at them, never acted like he was irritated with them.

Watching him was a treat. It was like being able to be on the outside looking in. Like watching the best family television show. He was dressed casually in a pair of khaki shorts and a loose T-shirt. Sometimes when he ran or dropped to the ground, his shirt would rise, exposing a stretch of skin. Every time I saw his flat stomach I thought about last night. He was a beautiful man. Every inch of him. I wanted to trace every muscle with my tongue. He turned to look at me, his eyes narrowed when he saw me looking at him. I bit my bottom lip. I knew he had a good idea about what I was thinking about. I didn't care. I let him see the want, hoping to spark the same in him.

He shot me a look that said *not today*. Hell, maybe the look said *not ever*. It was a small blow to my ego. I wasn't going to let it get me down. I wasn't going to give up. He'd gone through hell to get back to me. I had to put in some fight.

"Not again!" I heard him shout before bursting into laughter.

Mitchell was wrapped around one leg with Ellie around his other one, trying to take him to the ground.

"Get him!" Ellie cried out.

"Nooo," Jacob cried out, struggling to stay standing.

I burst into laughter, watching as he fell to the grass. The kids piled on top of him, laughing and screaming with joy. It made my heart happy to see him playing with all the kids. He'd been a little stiff and tense at first, but my three little munchkins could make anyone laugh. I had never seen Jacob laugh like he was. He looked like he was truly enjoying himself. I loved watching him with Ellie. Every mama wanted her baby to have a good daddy. Jacob was going to be a damn good daddy.

"I want a horse ride!" Ellie shouted.

I groaned, feeling horrible that he was being tortured. I had never seen anyone, not my dad, Philip, or Larry ever play with them like Jacob was. He was acting like one of them. His boundless energy surprised me. The kids could be exhausting. Very few people had been able to keep up with them. I could see them slowing down but knew they would fight it every step of the way. When they ran that hard, they crashed hard. If they didn't get a few minutes to lie down, they turned into little, cranky beasts. It always led to lots of squabbling and made me want to pull my hair out. I could see them flagging and knew it was time to step in. I hated to stop the fun, but it was either stop it or deal with the meltdowns that were sure to follow.

"All right, guys, let's take care of those water bottles and load up," I said.

"What? Why?" Ellie protested. "We're still playing."

It was the beginning of the whining stage. I knew it well. I knew it well enough to know I didn't want to live through it if it was avoidable. Mackenzie chimed in; her lower lip pushed out in a pout.

I looked at Jacob, who appeared ready to put forth his own protest. "It's time to go home. It's time for a N-A-P," I said in a low voice, my eyes widening as I jerked my head, trying to talk without saying the words.

The girls burst into giggles. I turned to look at Mitchell. He had his little hand smacked against his forehead, slowly shaking it back and forth, looking like a miniature version of his father. "Something wrong?" I asked him.

"I'm six, not two. I can spell," he said with a great deal of exasperation. "We don't need naps. We're big kids."

I raised my eyebrows, trying to fight back my own laughter. Sometimes, he could sound like a forty-year-old man. I cleared my throat. "I'm sorry. You're right. I think it's time to go home and settle in for a little TV time. You guys need some quiet time," I said in a stern, monotone voice as if we were negotiating a business deal.

Quiet time was code for nap. They were older and didn't take regular naps, but after running as hard as they did earlier, I had a feeling quiet time would lead to a few power naps.

"You want us to take a nap," he protested.

I shook my head. "Nope. I want you guys to take a little break. If you fall asleep, that's okay; if not, that's fine," I said doing my best to sound completely reasonable.

"I could use a little quiet time as well. You guys are hard to keep up with," Jacob told them.

"We want to play a little more," Ellie protested.

"I think you guys can play again another time," I said, looking at Jacob to see if he was willing to do that.

He nodded. "I'd love to play tag again. Maybe next week we'll have another picnic."

"Are you going to bring tuna sandwiches this time?" Ellie questioned.

Jacob grinned. "I will. With pickles."

"Yeah!" Ellie cheered.

"Alright, let's get a move on," I said, slapping my hand against the table and getting to my feet.

The kids got up and dragged their feet as they made their way back to the SUV. With Jacob's help, we got them buckled in without a lot of complaints. Judging by the exhausted looks on their faces, I had a feeling they would all be passed out before I even made it outside of town. I used the remote start to turn on the engine and get the AC blowing before closing the door.

Jacob was standing there, his hands in his pockets as he stared through the back-passenger window. "She's a handful," I said quietly.

He nodded his head. "She is."

"I hope they weren't too much for you," I joked, trying to lighten the mood a bit.

"They weren't. Thank you for letting me spend some time with her. I'd like to do it again," he said, his voice stiff and lacking emotion.

I nodded. "I think that would be a good idea. She'd love to. Jacob, you did great with her today," I told him with a smile.

He was going out of his way to keep his distance from me. His hands were shoved deep in the pockets of his khaki shorts. He'd put on his sunglasses, blocking his eyes, adding another wall between us.

"I need to get going," he replied, moving to step past me.

"Jacob—"

He looked at me, his jaw set. "Not now."

I nodded, understanding he was telling me he didn't want to talk about us. "Okay. Um, should I call you?"

"For?" he asked.

I gulped down the lump in my throat. "We need to finalize the details for the ice cream social."

"I'll handle it."

"I see. I guess you'll let me know when you'd like to see Ellie again?" I asked hopefully.

He smirked. "Yes, that I will let you know."

He walked around the front of his truck and got into the cab without even looking my way. He pulled out of the parking lot, leaving me standing there staring at his taillights. I had screwed up. He was different. Last night he'd at least wanted me. In the bright light of day, he couldn't even look at me. He was giving me the cold shoulder.

I took a deep breath, pushing down the sadness. I got into the SUV, a bright, fake smile on my face as I pulled out of the parking lot. Inside, I could feel my heart shattering. He'd professed his love for me, claimed he wanted a relationship and he was willing to fight for it. I had rejected his advances. I had told him we couldn't be together, but today, watching him with all of the kids in the park, I let myself have a little fantasy.

I let myself dream about a future with the three of us as a family. I imagined us having dinner together and spending our weekends playing at parks and going camping or visiting various other family adventures. I felt like an idiot for thinking he would run out on us when he found out about her. I should have known better. I had cut him deep. It was a cut I didn't think was going to heal anytime soon. I knew his history. He didn't have a family. He didn't have anyone in his corner. He'd always been on his own, and when we had gotten together, he'd had a lot of walls and a giant chip on his shoulder. It had taken me years to get him to open up, to be my friend, to let me see who he really was.

I hated to think I had lost him for good. He'd just come back in my life, just given me hope for a future, and now I had ruined that.

"Why?" I whispered, slapping the steering wheel.

"What, Mom?" Ellie asked from the back seat.

"Nothing, sweetie," I said, choking back the tears.

I had to hold it together until I got them settled in. Then, I would take a three-minute bathroom break and cry my heart out. It was hard to fathom my life had been turned upside down and inside out just because I had opened the front door at the Welsh mansion. Everything had changed in that moment. I had run the full gamut of emotions from happy to furious to heartbroken. I wasn't great at the chase. I had chased him for years back in high school—*years*. It had taken me years to get him to want me. I didn't want to wait that long again.

I parked the car, got the kids unloaded, and ushered them into the living room. I put on one of their favorite movies and passed out the plush blankets—even though it was hot as sin outside, the AC in the mansion was always on overtime. I busied myself in the living room, waiting to see if they were officially settled or if there was going to be a round of demands. When no one asked for water or a snack, I snuck off to the bathroom and let myself have that cry.

## 27

## JACOB

Things were kind of in a holding pattern at work, leaving very little for any of us to actually do. All the applications for permits were filled out and waiting until we felt we would get the green light before we ever filed. Plans were drawn up and waiting. Everything was waiting. The town council wasn't budging. The ice cream social was essentially our last hope. Erin was going to be a huge part of that. I needed to set aside my differences with her and get her back on the team.

I wasn't going anywhere. I was going to be staying in Burning Butte, and it would make life easier if I had a good job to support my daughter. I was one half of a family. It was strange to think of myself as a family man, but I was. Or at least, I was going to be. I was in Ellie's life for good, come hell or high water. She was stuck with me. I couldn't believe Erin ever thought I would walk away from my child. She had to think I was some kind of monster.

Truth was, I didn't think I could walk away from either one. I was pissed at Erin, but I loved her. I'd always loved her, and that love didn't stop when I found out she'd been keeping a secret. I'd been hurt, cut to the core, but I didn't hate her. It hurt so bad because I did love her. The looks she'd given me at the park and the silent pleading for attention had been difficult to ignore. My reaction at the park had been more about me wanting to punish her for the pain she had caused me than any actual dislike of her. I loved her. That hadn't changed. It wouldn't change.

There was a lot of shit to work through, no matter what happened between us. I owed her an apology for the cold-shoulder treatment and a few of the things I had said to her. I wanted us to be together, and I hated the idea of wasting precious time being mad at her for something that was all done and over. Truthfully, the secret ended up being the best gift in the world. I couldn't be mad at her for giving me a daughter.

Philip was the last man standing in my way of getting my happily ever after, or at least close to it. It was about time he and I had our face-to-face. He seemed to be avoiding me, or maybe I was avoiding him. Regardless, it was time to let the guy know I wasn't going anywhere. Erin had the idea things would eventually just get better, but I didn't want to wait. I didn't like the idea of Philip hanging over my head.

I closed down my computer, grabbed my keys, and left the relatively empty offices of Western Energies. We had put everyone on hiatus while we worked to figure out the situation with the permits. I drove straight to the sheriff's office, hoping to find Philip there.

"Hi," I greeted the older woman sitting behind a desk out front.

"I remember you," she replied.

I grinned. "Good. I'm here to see Sheriff Maxwell. Is he in?"

The woman looked skeptical. "Are you going to start trouble?"

I raised an eyebrow, studying her close before I remembered who she was. "You're working for the sheriff's department, Mrs. Munch?" I asked my former math teacher with surprise.

"I retired from teaching. Too many hoodlums like you coming through my doors," she said with a laugh.

Mrs. Munch had been a good teacher, but I hated math and school, and I had been a rebellious shit. Out of all my teachers, she'd probably been the most understanding, but she'd been strict. She'd given me detention more than anyone else.

"Don't shoot me," I teased.

"Philip's in his office," she said, jerking her thumb toward the door behind her.

"Thank you."

I knocked once and pushed open the door. I knew if he knew it was me, he wouldn't invite me in. It probably wasn't the smartest thing in the world to confront an armed man, but I was going to do it anyway. Philip looked up from the report he was working on and dropped the pen. He stood up, his hands going to his hips as he stared me down.

"What are you doing here?" He glowered at me.

"I'm here to talk, and you're damn well going to listen," I

said, taking a seat in the hard wooden chair across from his desk.

"I have nothing to say to you," he snapped, taking his seat.

"Good, because I just said you're going to be doing the listening, I'm going to be doing the talking. There is some stuff to work out, and it's about time we did that."

Philip sneered, shaking his head. "I don't care what you have to say, but you must be pretty fucking stupid to walk right into the lion's den."

I shrugged a shoulder, not the least bit concerned by his bluster. That was classic Philip. "You're going to listen anyway."

"What? What do you want?"

"I know about Ellie. I know Erin and I have a daughter together, and I know you and your dad and everyone else in this town thought it was a good idea to keep that from me. Well, too late and too bad. I'm here to stay and I'm not leaving my daughter ever again. Now that I know about her, no one—not you, your dad, or the whole damn town—is going to run me out. If I go, she goes," I said firmly, looking him dead in the eye.

Philip stared back at me. "You shouldn't have a daughter. You should have never done what you did."

"I do and I did. You need to get over yourself, Philip. Erin and I had—*have*—something special. I don't know why that is so hard for you to understand. She wasn't a little girl when we got together. She's old enough to make her own decisions now, and she was then," I told him.

"She's my little sister. You know I didn't want you messing with her," he said, sounding frustrated.

I nodded. "I know and I am sorry about that, but it wasn't me 'messing with her.' I cared for her deeply back then, and I still do. She's the one woman in the world I want to be with. I'm sorry it ruined our friendship, but she means more to me than you did."

He scoffed. "How do you know that? She was eighteen and you were twenty-one. There is no way it could have been that serious."

"It was and it still is. I came back for her, and I don't plan on leaving; especially now that I know about Ellie," I said firmly. "What you did back then, it wasn't cool. You acted rashly, and you cost me and your sister a lot."

Philip looked down at his desk. "I didn't know she was pregnant."

"But you knew she loved me."

"She was a kid. She didn't know what love was."

I shook my head. "She did. I did. I'm back, Philip. You can either give us your blessing or get out of the way, but I won't let you interfere this time."

He was quiet for a few minutes. "She was really hurt when she found out what we did."

"Of course she was. You and your dad were smothering her. You refused to accept she had grown up," I said.

He nodded. "I always felt like I had to look out for her. She didn't have a mom to talk to. She didn't really talk to me about stuff like that. When I found out you two had been sneaking off together, I was furious. I saw red. You didn't exactly have a stellar reputation back then. I thought Erin could do so much better. I didn't want her getting side-tracked from her goals by the town troublemaker."

"I wasn't the town troublemaker alone. You were with me for a lot of those acts," I reminded him.

"I know."

"She's a smart girl. You need to trust her when she tells you what she wants," I advised.

"Erin needed someone who could take care of her and give her all the things in life my dad couldn't. I wanted her to be able to move away and live in a big house and go to school or do whatever she wanted. I didn't see her getting that with you," he said.

His words stung a little, but I knew they were the truth. "I get it, I do, and that's why I've been working my ass off so I could give her everything she wants and needs. I'll make sure Ellie is well taken care of too."

"If I would have known she was pregnant, things probably would have been a little different," he grumbled.

I laughed. "Like you would have disposed of my body?" I joked.

He grinned. "Basically. I did consider hunting you down after I found out she was having your baby." He got a serious look on his face, shaking his head. "She was my little sister," he whispered.

I winced. I did feel guilty about that one little fact. "I'm sorry. I didn't mean for it to happen. I don't know how much she has told you, but we had been kind of seeing each other for years before anything ever happened. I fought my attraction for her. I told her repeatedly we couldn't be together because of you, but your sister is tenacious. The entire time I was pushing her away, I was falling in love with her. I loved her. I wouldn't have hurt her. I wanted to talk to you about my feelings for her, but you made it very clear you would never accept me as her boyfriend."

"This isn't an easy situation. I know you're trying to buy a house. I know you're planning on sticking around and that means we have to figure out how to live in the same town without killing each other," he grumbled.

"Philip, I don't want to kill you. I don't hate you. I'm pissed at what you cost me, but it's in the past. I want to move forward. I would like it if we could get along for Erin and Ellie's sake. Your dad seems to accept me—don't you think it's about time you figured out how to do the same?" I asked.

"There's a lot of water under the bridge," he said.

I shrugged a shoulder. "Not mine. I'm over it. I have a bright future ahead of me. I don't really give a shit if you can forgive me. I'm forgiving you. I'm moving on. You can wallow in the past and get mad and try to stir up shit, but you're not going to get at me. I refuse to play games. I lost eight years with Erin and Ellie, and I don't plan on losing another day. I'm here. I'm not leaving, and you can either deal with it or sit here and stew. I don't care."

"Do you really think you can waltz back into town and everything is going to be all rainbows and butterflies?" he snapped.

I chuckled at his analogy. "It has never been rainbows and

butterflies, but I'm not giving up." I got to my feet and gave him a last look. "It was good seeing you, Philip. Congratulations on the job. I wish you all the happiness in the world."

I left his office, not waiting for his reply. It wasn't exactly a good talk, but I sure as hell felt better. We weren't going to be hugging it out anytime soon, but I felt like we had come to an understanding. Time would tell if we would ever be friends again. That was on Philip. I was turning my focus and energy elsewhere.

# 28

## ERIN

I closed my eyes, completely relaxed with the sun heating my exposed skin in the bikini I had put on. The kids were at an outdoor school for the day, and the Welshes had taken off for a second, or third, or maybe even a fourth honeymoon. I was completely and totally alone, something that happened almost never. I was soaking it up by laying out by the pool in the bikini I had bought last summer but was too embarrassed to wear around the kids. It gave Ivy's bikini a run for the money in the sexy and revealing department.

When Larry and Ivy asked if they could double my pay for the week if I agreed to watch the kids all week while they "reconnected," I happily agreed to do it. I was happy to see them getting along better. I told them I didn't need the money, but they'd insisted. It was hard to imagine I was getting paid to lounge by the pool.

I stretched my legs, pointing my toes and adjusting my body on the lounge chair. I had on my sunglasses and sunhat and was on the verge of dozing off. The sun was like a tranquilizer and had lulled me into complete relaxation. I could certainly see the appeal to become a beach bum on some warm Florida beach or maybe some tropical destination.

I heard something, something that didn't fit with the tranquility of the backyard. I turned my head, trying to identify the sound, and saw a shadowy figure. I squealed, sitting up and reaching for the towel I had dropped on the cement beside me. And then I realized it was Jacob. He was wearing dark sunglasses and a suit, looking very men-in-black as he strolled across the patio toward me.

"What are you doing here? How did you get in?" I asked with confusion.

He shrugged a shoulder, standing over me. "I hopped the fence."

"You hopped the fence? Again?"

His sexy grin sent a shiver down my spine. "Yes."

I shook my head. "It seems to be habit with you."

"Old habits die hard, and I only jump when I really need to talk to you. Like now. I'm completely sober this time," he said, grabbing one of the other chairs and dragging it closer to mine.

I sat up, putting my bare feet on the warm cement and watching as he sat down on the edge of the chair, our knees brushing against one another. "Talk to me?" I asked, somewhat worried about what he was going to say.

He slowly nodded. I couldn't see his eyes through the dark lenses but imagined they were that same intense gaze I had seen at the park that day.

"We need to talk about how we are going to be the best co-parents to Ellie," he said, his voice devoid of emotion.

"Oh," I choked out.

He pushed up his sunglasses. I quickly did the same, sensing what he was about to say was something that needed to be said with full eye contact. My stomach churned with nervousness. I felt flushed and jittery as his gaze bored into mine. He was so damn intense he was making me nervous enough to puke.

"I have a plan," he started. "The best way to be co-parents is to do it like it was intended."

"Oh?" I squeaked.

"I think we need to live in the same house. I don't want to shuffle her back and forth. If we're going to be living together, we may as well take advantage of the tax breaks and get married. That way we all have the same last name and she won't have to explain the very unique situation to her friends as she gets older. We'll be able to save money by splitting the costs, and we won't have to spend extra money on gas transporting her from one house to the other," he explained as if he were proposing a business deal.

I was going to puke. I slapped a hand over his mouth, demanding he stop talking before I truly did lose my lunch. "Stop. Don't say another word," I said, shaking my head. "Your plan, it's a plan. It's a business model. It's functional and smart and completely devoid of feeling. There's no love, no romance. I don't—"

He pulled my hand away from his mouth, a smile on his lips as he looked at me. "Erin, be reasonable," he cajoled.

My eyebrows shot up. "Reasonable? Seriously? Reasonable? Is that how you are going to approach life? Is that what you're going to tell Ellie she should look for in a relationship? Be reasonable?" I shrieked, fury pumping through my veins.

He shrugged a shoulder. "I'm going to be making good money, assuming we get the stupid permits through," he grumbled. "I can provide for you and Ellie. You can be a full-time mom or go back to school or do whatever you want. I can keep a roof over your head and food on the table and make sure Ellie has a stable place to call home."

I shook my head in complete disbelief. "And us? Do we date other people?"

"We'll be married," he said simply.

"Married for convenience. I can't—"

He put a finger to my lips. "Shh, don't say it."

I twisted my head to the side. "No. I will not—"

He grabbed my arm and yanked me over the expanse between us, pulling me into his lap and cradling me. "Erin, I love you. I've never stopped loving you. I want you. I want the total package. I want to be with you. I want to marry you and raise our child—children," he added. "You are all I want. You are all I need. I can't get through this life without you."

"But—"

My question died on my lips when he pressed his mouth to mine. His arms held me close to him as his mouth worked over mine. I could feel a tear of joy and relief slide down my cheek. He pulled back a few inches, looking into my eyes as he rubbed his thumb over my cheek. "Tears?" he asked in a quiet voice.

"Happy tears," I whispered.

"Where are the kids?" he asked in a husky voice.

"Gone for a couple more hours," I told him, feeling that familiar pull of desire.

"Good. Anyone else here?"

I gave a small shake of my head. "No."

"Good," he growled, squeezing my thigh. "I hate the idea of you wearing this skimpy little thing around other men."

I chuckled. "I wouldn't dare. This is my tanning suit I only wear when I know I have privacy, which is never, until today."

"I like it, but I like you naked even better," he said, causing a million goose bumps to erupt over my skin.

"We're alone," I reminded him.

He grinned. "You said that. Do you want me to kiss you?" he whispered, giving me a soft kiss on my lips. "Touch you like this?" he asked, running his hand over my breast barely covered by the vibrant blue triangle of fabric I was wearing.

I whimpered, adjusting myself on his lap. "Yes, touch me."

"I want to touch you, but I think we should maybe go inside for this."

"Okay. Upstairs," I said, jumping off his lap.

I grabbed my phone and padded barefoot across the patio, anxious to get the man inside. I had electricity humming through my body. I turned to see if he was following and stopped moving when I saw him still standing next to the chair. "What are you doing?" I asked, wondering if he had changed his mind.

He grinned. "Watching you walk away in the sexiest bikini I have ever seen."

The way he was looking at me, like I was on the menu at one of the best restaurants in the world, gave me confidence. Without thinking, I reached behind me, unhooked the clasp of the bikini top, and dropped it to the ground. He reached down and adjusted himself, his gaze on my bare breasts. He made no move to come toward me. Feeling completely emboldened, I hooked my finger in the tiny bottoms and pushed them down my legs, bending over and very carefully pulling them over my feet before tossing them on top of the bikini top and standing fully erect. I stared at him. In that moment I was completely stripped down in every sense of the word. I was giving myself to him. I was vulnerable and exposed.

He slowly moved toward me, his hand reaching for his tie and pulling it off before tossing it onto the cement. He ripped open his shirtfront, casting it to the side and coming to stand in front of me. I looked up at him, feeling so small in my naked state.

"You're the most beautiful woman in the world, and you're mine," he said, putting one finger under my chin.

I slowly nodded. "I'm yours."

"Baby?" he whispered, his mouth hovering just above mine.

"Hmm?" I murmured, completely lost in the moment.

"I need to get you into bed. Where are the damn stairs?" he growled.

I smiled, leaned up on my toes, and gave him a quick kiss before spinning around and walking toward the side door. I could hear his heavy footsteps behind me. He reached out once and squeezed my ass, groaning loud. I picked up the pace. I was so hot and ready for him I feared I would climax on my up the stairs.

I pushed open the door to my apartment and turned to face him. He closed the door behind him and immediately undid his pants, stripping naked before coming to stand in front of me. He reached up and cupped my face, his thumb brushing across my cheek as he stared into my eyes with such love and tenderness I almost started weeping. I could feel his love for me. It infused me with warmth and pleasure and made me want to curl up in his arms and never step away.

His mouth covered mine, a sweet kiss full of hope and promise as our bodies melded together. I reached up, sliding my hands up his strong back. I held him with comfort in the knowledge he was mine. He was my man, and I wasn't ever going to let him go. Touching him felt different. It was different knowing he was mine. I knew without a doubt nothing would ever come between us. We'd fought to get to the point where we were, and I was going to hold on to him with every ounce of strength I had.

"Bedroom," he muttered against my lips.

I walked backward, pulling him with me as he continued to kiss me. I nearly stumbled over a stray shoe in the hall, but his arms were there to catch me. We made it to my room with no injury. I climbed on top of my bed, ready for him to love me with his body.

He crawled in beside me and gently pushed me onto my back. His hand caressed over my chest as he watched with such intensity it made goose bumps spread out over my body once again. He cupped my breast, holding it up as he gently closed his mouth over my nipple. A soft whimper escaped my lips as he worked his mouth over my body.

"You taste so good. I want to taste every inch of you," he whispered.

I opened my eyes and looked down just in time to see him dive between my legs. The next several minutes blurred as he took me to a place of such exquisite ecstasy, I knew I would never be the same again.

# 2 9

## JACOB

I wanted to brand her with my tongue and set out to do exactly that. I kissed every inch of her body, right down to her toes and paying very special attention to the area between her legs. With two orgasms for her, I made my way back up to her mouth, kissing her and letting her know in no uncertain terms she was mine forever.

"Always and forever," I whispered against her lips. "You will be mine always and forever," I repeated.

Her eyes, slightly glazed over, stared back at me. "Always and forever."

I reached between my legs, guided myself to her slick opening swollen from the two climaxes, and pushed in gently at first. She was so tight and wet, I nearly exploded before I even got more than a couple of inches inside her sweet body.

She let out a long, satisfied moan as I slid deeper inside, seating myself fully inside her. I held my weight off her, using one hand to brush the hair back from her brow, slick with perspiration. I smiled, looking down into her face and feeling such complete happiness I could do nothing else except smile. She smiled back at me.

I dropped my lips to hers, meaning to give her a quick kiss, but her body squeezed around mine, sending a jolt of fire through me. My kiss intensified and I began to move. Need drove me on to pump in and out of her body until I was suddenly desperate, frantic for the release I had craved since the last time I had her.

"Oh god," I groaned, the orgasm rolling over me like a steamroller, gripping my body and straining every muscle as I exploded inside her.

Her soft whimpers turned to cries of pleasure as she joined me in ecstasy. I held myself off her as the spasms rocked through both of us for a full minute after the orgasms. I dropped beside her, already missing her snug warmth around me, and pulled her into my arms. She felt so right next to me. I couldn't imagine ever holding anyone close to me other than her. She was made for me. I knew that as surely as I knew my own name.

"You know, I've always had a thing for you, even when I wasn't supposed to. It wasn't necessarily a sexual attraction I felt, but I liked being around you. Your happiness and easygoing nature just pulled me in. It was truly like a magnetic attraction. Whenever I would come by the house, I would feel drawn to be in the same room as you," I told her.

"I felt the same way."

"I want it to be clear I never, ever had any creepy sexual thoughts about you when you were fifteen, sixteen, and whatever. I know your brother thinks that is what it was, but I swear, it wasn't a sexual attraction. It was just... I don't know. It was like I loved you with my heart and nothing more," I explained, feeling like I was completely making a mess of things.

She giggled softly, turning her face up to look at me. "You loved me. You loved me like a friend. You cared about me. I think that's why what we have is special. We knew each other before there was any of the feelings. It was a love fueled by our friendly feelings. I do get it. I don't care if Philip gets it. It was like my heart recognized you as my other half before I even knew your name. I was drawn to you as well."

I laughed, rubbing my hand over her arm. "You know, I would have been okay being friends with you for a lot longer. I just loved hanging out with you, but damn if you didn't start putting thoughts in my head with all the flirting and those stolen kisses. A man only has so much self-control."

Her laughter filled the room. "You were a much bigger person than I was, literally and figuratively. I developed a crush on you almost instantly. You were the bad boy, the brother's best friend, and the boy I was not supposed to like. I was not as strong as you were and was not inclined to fight my feelings for you. I wanted you and I was determined to have you."

I rolled my eyes. "You were a feisty thing. No matter how many times I told you no, you kept coming back. I remember that time you told me you needed help taking out the trash. It was a setup! You pushed me up against the fence and kissed me."

"You kissed me back," she pointed out.

"Yes, only because I had no choice. I was afraid you would maul me!"

She slapped at my chest. "Liar. You wanted me."

"I wanted you, but you were the forbidden fruit. I wasn't supposed to want you. I cannot tell you how many nights I would leave your house after some of those sneaked kisses and have such a hard-on it would hurt," I complained.

She burst into a fit of giggles. "Honestly, back then, I never really understood any of that. It wasn't like my dad and brother had the birds and the bees talk with me. I just knew I liked the way you made me feel, and I really loved kissing you and touching your body."

"You nearly killed me," I complained. "There was no way I could resist you forever. Part of me knew I either had to give in to it or leave town. I didn't want to leave. Ironic that giving in to what I felt for you was exactly the thing that had me leaving town."

"I'm sorry for the way all that happened. Again, I was so naïve. I think I had this idea in my head that nothing could possibly go wrong if we were together. That first time, I went home and felt like I was the luckiest woman on the planet. It was always supposed to be you," she said, her voice soft.

"I did feel very lucky to be with you. I had thought about how I was going to tell Philip I wanted to be with you. The night they came to me, I had finally worked up the courage to tell him I was in love with you. He didn't give me a chance. They came at me with guns blazing, so to speak.

They didn't care what I had to say. They treated me like I had snatched a little girl from their house. It was one of the worst days of my life," I told her, closing my eyes and thinking back to the moment I knew I wouldn't see her again. It had damn near killed me.

"I'm sorry," she whispered. "I should have been more careful. They heard me talking on the phone to Marianne. It was not a good scene at my house either."

"You know I would have fought to my death if I had known about the baby, right?"

She nodded, her cheek sliding up and down my chest. "I do know that."

"Good."

"You were always the man I saw in my future. You know when you close your eyes and you think about where you'll be in ten years or whatever? You. You were always there. I would dream about meeting, falling in love, getting married, and raising a family. It was always you, me, and our family living happily and peacefully," she said on a sigh. "Never once was I able to think of myself with anyone else. I did try, don't get me wrong. I never thought I would see you again, but no matter how hard I tried, it was always your face I saw."

"I'm here. You will see my face every damn day whether you like it or not. Our little fantasy might be done a bit out of order, but I'm determined to start fresh, from square one. We already have the kid, and now we need to make us a family with the big house and the white picket fence," I promised her.

She groaned. "You're a fool. A white picket fence?"

"I'm a fool in love with you, baby, and I will paint the damn fence blue if it suits you. I want the total package. I want the dream. You know what I'm talking about. We spent hours planning our future. That's the future I want. Those weren't just fantasies. We can make them realities," I vowed.

"Jacob Miner, you are such a romantic!"

"Damn straight, and it's all because of you. You make me feel cheesy and like I can have all those things. I wouldn't even dare to dream about any of it if you weren't the one by my side. I wouldn't want any of it. You're all that I want. You and Ellie are all I need in this life. If Western Energies falls apart, I'll get a job bucking hay. I don't care what I have to do, but I will do it to keep you happy. I will do anything for you and our daughter," I told her vehemently.

She was quiet—too quiet. I looked down at her and saw a tear slide down her face. I wiped it away again and held her close. I knew exactly how she felt. I wasn't one for tears, but I knew the overwhelming emotions she was feeling. I had felt them too when I realized I had always known what I wanted. I'd been a little waylaid by the blow I had a child, but as soon as the shock wore off, I knew.

I held her close, both of us quiet for several minutes. I heard her let out a long sigh. "Thank you."

"For?"

"For accepting me and my many flaws. I'd like to promise I'll never screw up, but I have a feeling I will. I just need you to know I will always love you and you are my north star. I will always follow you and know I'm going the right way. You're all I will ever need."

I continued stroking her arm. "When do you have to pick up the kids?" I asked.

"Two hours."

I pulled away from her, leaning my head on my elbow as I looked down at her. "Good. Because what I'm going to do to you over the next ninety minutes or so requires complete privacy," I said, gazing into her eyes.

I saw her shudder. "What you're going to do to me?" she whispered.

I slowly nodded. "I'm going to make you scream my name. You're going to be a limp noodle by the time I finished with you. I have eight years to make up for. Eight fucking years of cold, lonely nights with nothing but my hand for company. I want to bury myself so deep inside your body you can't think straight. I want you writhing and whimpering as I fuck you into complete oblivion."

She moaned, licking her lips. "You're going to make me come with your words alone."

"Good. I'm going to give you so many orgasms you lose count."

# EPILOGUE

## ERIN - ONE MONTH LATER

I slid the lightweight dress over my head, letting the fabric fall over my body. My skin felt electric, a side effect I had been dealing with quite a bit over the last few weeks. Jacob had been very serious when he said he wanted to make up for lost time. I wasn't sure if it was possible to have too much pleasure, but I was beginning to feel like I was always aroused. He was always pulling me away for quickies during the middle of the day. I would stop by his office after dropping the kids off at school, and it always ended up with us in his private bathroom or on his desk. We were planning on moving in together next week, but in the meantime, we had stealthy sleepovers. I suspected Larry and Ivy knew, but I wasn't quite ready to explain any of that to Ellie and the Welsh kids.

"Want any help?" Jacob asked, letting himself into my room.

I turned and looked at him, shaking my head. "No. Don't you dare. I just got dressed."

He grinned, walking to me and putting his hands on my hips, rubbing his pelvis against me. "Ellie is downstairs with the Welsh's. We don't have to be there for another hour. We've got time."

"Jacob!" I gasped when he lifted the fabric of my sundress and rubbed between my legs.

"Look at that, you're already wet," he said with that sexy grin of his that always made me want him.

I groaned. "I'm always like that. I feel like a nymphomaniac."

"I don't mind it one bit. One quickie. All it will take is a quick in and out." His voice was husky as he kissed along my neck, his fingers working magic between my legs.

We both knew I wasn't going to deny him. He was right: it had taken less than five minutes for us to reach fulfillment. I quickly dressed and fixed my makeup, and together we headed into the mansion, finding the family in the living room. I blushed when Ivy looked my way, grinning from ear to ear with that knowing look on her face.

"Are we ready to go?" Larry asked, getting to his feet.

"Let's do this," Jacob agreed.

Ellie and I rode with Jacob, following behind the Welsh family as we headed out to one of the community churches that had let us use their facility for the ice cream social.

"Look!" Ellie exclaimed, pointing out the window at the assortment of bounce houses set up in the lawn.

I winked at him. "I guess you were right," he said.

"You know it. This will keep the kids occupied while the adults talk. Plus, with all the ice cream those kids are going to be consuming, they're going to need to bounce off some of that energy," I told him.

He parked the truck in the gravel parking lot alongside the church, leaving the paved parking lot for the townspeople we were hoping would show up to the ice cream social. There was so much riding on this one event. It was a lot of pressure, and I knew I could be out of a job if it wasn't a success. Not just me, but Jacob. We'd already agreed we would consider moving away from Burning Butte in order for him to get a good job. I wouldn't mind a change in scenery. I wasn't leaving him, and he wasn't leaving me; that one simple fact made it a little easier to think about our future.

We went inside, leaving Ellie with Ivy at the bounce houses while I checked on the ice cream situation. Larry and Jacob were huddled together, I assumed talking about their plan of attack. I was confident Jacob would be accepted back in the fold. My dad had made it clear he was a part of the family, and Philip was slowly coming around. Jacob was a likeable guy, and if people gave him a chance, they would love him.

"It looks amazing. Thank you for all your hard work on this," Larry said, coming to stand in front of the table that had every kind of ice cream topper imaginable set out in pretty crystal bowls.

"You're welcome. I have a vested interest in you guys sticking around," I said with a laugh.

He smiled, nodding his head. "I appreciate all you've done

for me and my family. You know our door is always open if you need anything."

I smiled at him. "You've done a lot for me as well. Ellie and I are going to miss living upstairs, but I'm so happy you and Ivy are starting a new chapter in your life together."

"This will be good for her. She is ready to take a step back and focus on being a mom. She'll still be plenty busy with her other charities, and I thank you for agreeing to stay on part-time. If you need more work, you just holler and I'll make sure to get you something," he assured me.

I smiled, my eyes drifting to where Jacob was talking to a group of people that had come in. "I think I'm going to be okay. Jacob and I are going to start house shopping. Lord knows you pay him enough money to keep us comfortable," I said with a wink.

"Good. He's a good man, and I know he'll do right by you. You two are one of those couples that's going to last."

"You and Ivy are too," I assured him.

"We are now, thanks to your help. We found our way back together. I'm taking a step back at the company and letting Jacob put that fancy degree to work. I've missed too much time with my family. It's time to make them the center of my world instead of trying to make more money."

"That's good to hear. Now, don't look now, but you have some people approaching. I'll make the introductions, and then you're on your own. Ready?" I asked him.

He put on his most charming smile and gave me a wink. "Ready."

I quickly introduced him to some of the oldest citizens in Burning Butte and then left him to work his magic. I drifted outside to check on the kids, happy to see them playing and having fun. Ivy was surrounded by several women, all of whom seemed very happy to be talking to her. She looked like a queen, the attention all on her as she gushed on about her most recent charity event.

I made my way around the social, talking to people and doing my best to answer questions they had about Larry Welsh and the company, referring most of the questions about the company's plans to Jacob. I didn't want to screw up and say the wrong thing.

"Can I have everyone's attention please?" I heard Larry's voice come over the PA system. "Can everyone find a seat? I'd like to say a few words," Larry announced.

It took a few minutes, but the crowd found seats or huddled together along the outskirts of the community room of the church, their attention on Larry. I had butterflies in my stomach, knowing our futures in Burning Butte all depended on what he said next and how well it was received.

A warm arm wrapped around my shoulders. I looked up to see Jacob staring straight ahead, watching Larry with rapt interest. "It's going to be okay," I assured him.

"I hope so."

Larry held up his hand. "I'm Larry Welsh. If I haven't personally met you yet, please find me and let's shake hands. I want to thank all of you here in Burning Butte for showing up today. I know you all have a lot of questions and concerns, and I tell you what, that tickles my heart," he said, earning a chuckle from the crowd. "I don't know if you've all had a chance to meet my wife and kids, but if you haven't, I hope you'll find them as well. I'm a family man, and when I first visited Burning Butte, I knew it was the kind of place I wanted to raise my kids. I like the small-town feel and the laid-back, easy way the folks around here have. I went home and I told Ivy, we're moving. Now, it wasn't an easy move, and I will admit we are city slickers, but we fell in love with this place. We want to stay, and we join you in your concerns for the health and future of not only the town, but our families. Get with me or Jacob and we'd love to talk to you about our plans. You all have my word: I have only good intentions for Burning Butte."

I scanned the crowd, gauging their reactions to Larry's speech, and could see people liked him. They were receptive to what he was saying, which was a huge relief. I leaned up, putting my mouth close to Jacob's ear. "I think we better start looking for that house real soon, because your boss just secured your job."

He turned and grinned at me. "I think you're right. Why don't we celebrate with some ice cream? I've seen you eyeing those sundaes."

I giggled. "I think I would very much like some ice cream. I'm not nearly as nervous as I was."

"Good. Find a seat and I'll be right back. I'll grab Ellie too," he said, walking away from me.

I couldn't stop smiling as I watched him take Ellie's hand and head up to the tables where the ice cream was spread out. I found a seat at the end of one of the long tables and sighed with relief. Everything was going to be okay.

It wasn't long before Jacob and Ellie returned, carrying three ice cream sundaes complete with cherries on top. Ellie had a look on her face that told me she was up to something. I looked from Ellie to Jacob, who had a very similar expression, and knew for sure they were up to something.

"What'd you do?" I asked.

"Nothing!" Ellie squealed. "We brought you ice cream!"

I reached out to take one when Jacob pulled it away and gave me a different one. "This one is for you."

"Thank you," I said, putting it on the table and still watching them. "Are you going to sit down? You guys are making me nervous."

Ellie was still grinning like a fool. I looked down at the ice cream, wondering if it was covered with salt or something, and gasped. My mouth fell open, and tears filled my eyes as I looked up at Jacob. Ellie started giddily clapping her hands, attracting the attention of the others in the area.

Jacob, seeing me unable to move or speak, reached down and grabbed the diamond ring from its bed on of whip cream with a cherry in the center of it. He popped it in his mouth, sucked off the whip cream, and held it out to me. "I was hoping we could make this official. Will you marry me?" he asked, dropping to his knees in front of me.

"Oh yes! You know I will!" I exclaimed.

Ellie was bouncing and clapping. "I have a mommy and a daddy!" she squealed.

"You've always had a mommy and a daddy," I told her, tears streaming down my face.

"But now I have you both, together," she said, throwing her arms around me and hugging me before moving to hug Jacob.

"This is amazing. It's everything I always wanted. You did it. You made our dreams come true," I told him.

"You did it. You and I are partners for life. You dream it, I'll make it happen. I will give you the moon if you want it," he said, leaning in to give me a kiss.

An eruption of applause, cheers, and wolf whistles exploded around us. I felt my cheeks turn red. Jacob pulled me to a standing position and wrapped one arm around me and his other around Ellie as we all smiled at the crowd. We were a family—one very happy, whole family—and nothing would tear us apart.

Made in the USA
San Bernardino, CA
11 September 2019